BOUND TO THE ELF PRINCE

JESSICA GRAYSON
ARIA WINTER

Purple Fall
Publishing

DEDICATION

To my husband: You are not just my husband, you are my best friend and my rock. Thank you for all your love and support. I love you more than words can ever say.

-Jessica Grayson

CHAPTER 1

LYANA

Today is the day I have been dreading for over a year. I stand beside my father as a line of suitors wait outside the door, ready to present themselves for my hand.

It is my twenty-third birthday.

I sigh heavily. I should be celebrating with my friends, not receiving strangers who have come seeking marriage to a princess.

A tall man with short, brown hair and gray eyes approaches. He is dressed in full armor, although I suppose it is probably decorative. The metal is far too polished and unblemished to have ever seen battle. He flashes a handsome smile, and when he halts, I give him my best one in return.

I glimpse my reflection in his armor and barely recognize myself. The long, blue silk dress is lovely, but not something I would normally wear. The bodice is so tight I can barely breathe and is covered with an intricate pattern of clear crystals that trail down the length of the fabric. I try my best to ignore the discomfort of their hard, unforgiving pinch on my skin as I sit on my throne.

The color is a good contrast, however, to my long black hair, the light-brown eyes I inherited from my mother, and my red lips. My heavy crown makes it difficult to dip my chin and dismiss the handsome man, but I somehow manage. Because I must balance it so carefully atop my head, I sit rigidly, giving the illusion of a tall, proud figure when the truth is, I'm exhausted, and this process has only just begun.

While we wait for the next suitor to enter the room, Father leans in and whispers, "What did you think of Fredrik?"

At first, my mind is blank, until I realize he must be referring to the man who just left. I was so distracted by my uncomfortable attire that I wasn't paying attention when he gave us his name. "He has a good smile."

Father purses his lips, his dark-brown eyes searching mine. "That is all?"

I blink at him. "What else should there be? I know nothing about him beyond what I just saw in less than a minute."

"When he inherits his father's kingdom of Winterhold, he will be one of the wealthiest kings in all the realm. Their territory is known for gold and silver mines."

"Are we poor?"

Father's head jerks back. "What?"

"Is our kingdom heavily in debt?"

"Of course not," he scoffs. "Why would you think that?"

I shrug. "I thought perhaps that was why you were pushing me toward Fredrik."

He narrows his eyes. "Can a father not simply want his daughter to live in comfort? To never have to want for anything?"

"I live in comfort now," I counter. "I do not understand why I need to search for it elsewhere."

Father sighs and takes my stepmother's hand as she gives him a warm smile. "It is lonely to rule, Lyana. I merely wish to find someone to rule by your side. Fredrik would be a fine choice because of his wealth and his even temper."

"Your father is right, Lyana." My stepmother, Rina, takes my hand, her green eyes shining with kindness. We are only five years apart, but she has always seemed so much older and wiser. Perhaps it is because she was my tutor before she married my father. I have always valued her counsel. "You need a partner to shoulder such a heavy burden. I grew up in Winterhold. My family served the royal line for many generations. Prince Fredrik is an admirable person." She darts a glance at Father and smiles before winking at me. "It also does not hurt to have a handsome man at your side like I do."

Father tips his chin up smugly, and I arch a teasing brow. "Do not be telling him these things, Rina. You know how it goes to his head."

Father feigns indignation at my words while Rina and I laugh.

She inhales sharply, then stills before placing a hand over her rounded abdomen. Father's head snaps toward her in concern. "What is it?"

"Nothing," she replies. "The baby just moved, and it startled me."

My father rests his palm over her stomach, and his lips curve into a wide smile.

I'm so happy for them. Rina insists it will be a boy, but Father has repeatedly said he hopes for another girl. I suppose we'll have to wait and see.

The doors open, interrupting us as the announcer calls another suitor's name.

The next hour is a blur of faces and titles. Most of the

men are handsome and close to my age, though I'm not surprised to meet a few older ones as well. Our kingdom is prosperous, and I am the heir apparent. Whoever marries me will increase not only his lands but his wealth and status too.

As soon as the last man has presented himself, we escape into the next room.

Crowded with people, the grand ballroom is abuzz with a cacophony of voices. When we walk inside, they grow quiet and still, all eyes on us as we make our way down the center aisle toward a dais supporting three thrones.

My stepmother pauses and announces the beginning of the ball to celebrate my birthday. The crowd cheers. Each man I met earlier turns his gaze upon me now, already considering his best approach.

"What do you think, Lyana?" Rina warmly gestures to one of the many tables of food. "I had the kitchen make those lovely chocolate cakes you adore."

"Thank you, Rina."

She truly outdid herself preparing this ball. The golden chandeliers above us cast sparkling reflections on the polished stone floor. Long tables holding fluted glasses of bubbling champagne and goblets of wine line either side of the chamber. Behind them stand more tables, heavily laden with meats, cheeses, fruits, and bread, along with one solely dedicated to desserts. Men dressed in fine fabrics and women in elegant gowns whirl across the floor, keeping time with the enchanting music played by a string quartet in the corner.

A man approaches, and though his name escapes me, he looks familiar. I realize he is one of the suitors who has come seeking my hand—Prince Fredrik.

He bows low. "Princess Lyana, I wondered if I might have this dance."

I dart a glance at my father and stepmother. Rina nods encouragingly.

I stand. "I would be delighted," I lie. I am anything but.

Fredrik may be handsome, but something about his grin bothers me. It's too wide and toothy for my liking. But I remember now that he and his family are Wolf shifters, so I shouldn't be surprised.

I take his offered hand, and he pulls me onto the floor. I rest one hand on his shoulder as he holds my other. He places his free hand at my waist, but when he slides it around to the small of my back and drags me closer to him than is proper, I narrow my eyes and push him away. "I have changed my mind."

His mouth drops open, and I'm sure he plans to offer some excuse or other for his actions, but I dismiss him with a wave of my hand and return to my seat.

I have not yet sat down when the ballroom falls silent. Slowly, I spin to face the crowd, wondering what has caused the hush.

Dumbstruck, I blink at the main doors. An entourage of Elves is approaching. I shoot a confused look at Father, wondering if he was expecting them. His stunned expression assures me that he was not.

The banner they carry gives me pause. These are not just any Elves—they are High Elves from Rivenyl. We have engaged in many border disputes despite the treaty of nonaggression between our two kingdoms. With the latest border skirmishes, my father has feared the agreement will not hold, and now, I worry they bring demands that will end the peace.

One man leads the entourage. A silver circlet crowns his head, signifying he is royalty.

With broad shoulders that taper to a narrow waist, his lean muscular form is taller than any human man I've ever seen. If I had to guess, I believe the top of my head would barely be level with his chin.

He's dressed in a fine, dark-green tunic and pants, but his face draws my attention most, particularly his green, vertically slit pupils. My gaze travels over his short blond hair, the pointed tips of his ears, his aristocratic face, and his square, masculine jaw.

He approaches stoically and bows low. He lifts his head and his green eyes rake over my form with piercing intensity before returning to mine. "Princess Lyana of Eryadon, I am Prince Caelen of Rivenyl. I have come to seek your hand in marriage to seal a treaty between our people with a blood bond."

I'm so stunned by his offer, it takes me a moment to reply. "A blood bond?" I blurt, the question escaping my lips before I even realize I have spoken.

He nods, unshaken.

A frisson of fear runs down my spine. I can hardly believe his proposal. The idea of a blood bond is terrifying, to say the least. I have heard tales of how the Elves bond, and if they are true, the ritual is certainly nothing I would ever wish to try.

The room is watching us in awestruck silence. I cast a worried glance at my father.

He stands and moves toward Prince Caelen. "I believe we should continue this conversation in a more private setting."

Prince Caelen's gaze hardens even as he agrees.

Father turns to me and my stepmother. She places one hand protectively over her stomach while I take the other, and we all head back to the adjoining room.

Several of our guards surround us, forming a living wall between us and the Elven knights who protect Prince Caelen. As soon as we reach the private throne room and my father is seated, he addresses Caelen warily.

"Why do you come to us now? And why you, Prince

Caelen?" Father leans forward on his throne, narrowing his eyes. "You are the second-born son, asking for the hand of my daughter, who is heir to the throne. Where is your older brother, Dhurvaen?"

Caelen's eyes burn with anger and something else as he holds my father's gaze. "Dhurvaen is dead. He fell in battle against the Orcs."

My mouth falls open, and I recognize the other emotion that reflects behind his eyes—grief.

"My condolences on the loss of your brother," Father replies.

"Thank you. Dhurvaen's death is the reason I am here before you today." He pauses. "The Orcs are a common enemy of both our kingdoms. An alliance through marriage would strengthen our ability to stand against them."

Father straightens. "We already have a treaty of nonaggression with Rivenyl."

"This is true," Caelen replies. "But we both know how easily such agreements can be cast aside. An alliance through blood is stronger than any piece of paper."

My father sits back, considering. "My daughter is heir to this kingdom. Only *she* can decide if her husband would be king or merely consort."

Caelen stares at him, unwavering. "And I am heir to Rivenyl. I do not ask to be crowned ruler of Eryadon."

Caelen's gaze cuts to mine, and he steps forward. "I do not seek your throne. I ask for your hand in the hope of creating a permanent and lasting peace between our kingdoms."

He drops to one knee before me. In a swift motion, he pulls his blade from its sheath and draws the sharp edge across his palm. He bows low and presents the handle to me.

His green eyes pin me to the spot. "I give you my blade to protect and defend you always, and my blood to bind us as

7

one. I make this offering before the watchful eyes of the old gods. May their stars witness my vow as their silver light shines down upon me."

My mouth is dry as I study the blade.

Another Elf moves beside Caelen and bows low. "It is a tribute, Princess. Accepting the blade means you will consider Prince Caelen's proposal."

My heart slams in my throat as I reach forward and cautiously accept. The obsidian blood staining the metal reminds me that the man who would be my future husband is far from human.

Blue light flashes across the blade, and then dims. "Magic," I whisper, more to myself than anyone else.

Caelen's green eyes hold mine. "An unbreakable vow."

"And what if my daughter refuses you?" Father interrupts.

Caelen's head snaps up. "The magic is not binding until she accepts me as her mate. And if she does not, then more blood will undoubtedly be spilled along the borders of our lands. War will likely follow. Too much anger and hatred exist between your kind and mine. The Orcs use this to their advantage, seeking to keep us divided so they may conquer more lands unchecked. Only a match made in blood will heal the rift between our two kingdoms so we may stand against a common enemy."

Father holds his gaze. "We will consider your offer. I invite you to stay until we have made our decision."

Caelen nods.

Father turns to the guards. "Escort them to the guest wing."

Caelen stands to full height, tipping his chin to stare down imperiously. His emerald green, vertically slit pupils contract and then expand as they meet mine.

Fear steals my breath at his otherworldly and lethal

beauty. I curl my hands into fists and press them to my sides to still their trembling.

Caelen's gaze sweeps to my hands, his eyes flashing with an emotion I cannot discern while his face remains the perfect, impassive mask so typical of the High Elves.

He pivots and leaves with his guards. The moment the doors shut behind them, Rina clasps my hand, pulling me close as if to shield me. "She cannot marry him. Not a High Elf of Rivenyl. They are our sworn enemies."

"We have a treaty," Father replies. "They are *not* our enemies."

"Yes, they are," she protests, her voice shaking with anger. "How can you even consider it?"

"You think it is easy for me to consider offering my daughter's hand to a High Elf Prince?" Father clenches his jaw. "Every day I receive reports of yet another border skirmish between us. I may not like them, but the prince is right. The treaty we have on paper is not enough."

Despite his harsh words, I recognize the worry in his eyes as he regards me. "But a marriage between you might be the catalyst that moves us toward a permanent peace."

"It is not certain this will work," I counter.

"Nothing is certain, my daughter." Father's eyes shine with pity. "It is a risk. You might marry him and the fighting may continue and your sacrifice would be for nothing." He leans in and takes my hand. "But I know something the Elves do not."

"What is that?"

"That if anyone can lead us toward a path of peace, it is you. You are like your mother. She always had a head for politics, and she was one of the most selfless people I've ever known. I have never told you this, but I will tell you now. Your mother did not marry me for love. She married me to

9

ensure the peace between our two kingdoms. Love came for us much later. Perhaps it could for you as well."

"You cannot truly mean to sacrifice her to the High Elves," Rina interjects. "We discussed this. Prince Fredrik is the one we agreed she might—"

Father raises his hand in a bid for silence. "I know, my dear wife, but that was before Prince Caelen arrived. And I am not ceding her to the High Elves, I am leaving the choice up to her." He turns to me. "What say you, daughter of mine? What path will you choose?"

Father's words elicit a strange mixture of guilt, fear, and anger. He says it is my choice, but he already knows that there is none. A wise and just ruler always puts the needs of their kingdom and their people above their own.

I know in my heart what I must do, but that does not make the decision any easier. I glance down at the dagger in my hand—stained with the blood of my future husband.

Clenching my jaw, I meet his eyes evenly. "I will marry Prince Caelen of Rivenyl."

CHAPTER 2

CAELEN

As we proceed to the guest chambers, I cannot stop picturing the princess. With long hair as black as night, golden-brown eyes that glimmer like stars, and skin that appears touched by moonlight, she is captivatingly beautiful to behold.

I had not expected this. I heard humans could not come close to the beauty of our people, but it seems these rumors were wrong.

I had also not expected the fear in Lyana's eyes, nor the subtle trembling of her hands as her gaze met mine.

In her eyes, I am the enemy—a monster come to steal her and claim her as his bride. The thought burns like bitter acid on my tongue. I know she does not desire this marriage, but she understands the necessity for our kingdoms' benefit.

Both sides have lost many, and the death of my older brother, Dhurvaen, during battle with the Orcs, was a devastating blow felt throughout the kingdom.

The Orcs have an insatiable thirst for blood and war. If we are to have any chance of defeating their forces, we must have more allies. We cannot fight this war by ourselves.

A hand on my shoulder draws my attention, and I turn to find Ruvaen. His golden eyes hold wisdom. He has been my mentor since I was a child. He insisted upon accompanying me today, and I am glad for his presence.

"You presented yourself with honor today, my prince. Your brother would have been proud."

I swallow against the lump in my throat at the mention of Dhurvaen. I miss him. Every. Single. Day. "Thank you, Ruvaen."

When the Eryadon guards gesture me into my room, I'm surprised by the cramped space. I heard that humans build their castles differently from ours, but I never expected this. Instead of fine crystal or polished glass surfaces that reflect the soft glow of magic and candles, the walls are confining dark-gray stone, and the windows are little more than a square on each wall.

The castle was built for defense instead of aesthetics. Then again, since humans possess no magic, I suppose this was the rational choice.

Humans fear magic. As part of the treaty, they insisted that our powers be bound while we are in Eryadon. This bargain was sealed with the signing of the agreement between us.

I glance down at my hand and sigh heavily. It is strange to be unable to perform even a simple lighting spell to brighten these dreary chambers.

Furs and thick comforters form a deep layer atop the bed against the far wall. A fireplace beside it is already lit for warmth, and a table and chair sit across the way.

A door on the left wall leads to a cleansing room that is

sparsely decorated and utilitarian. Another heavy door opens onto a balcony overlooking the palace gardens. Compared to the gardens of my family's castle, these appear strange and unnatural. Every plant is arranged in neat rows and patterns, and the shrubbery trimmed into sharp angles and shapes. Beautiful flowers bloom from nearly every stem, but there is nothing wild or natural about this place.

The gardens of my home are as wild and untamed as the great forests that surround our capital. Our people have always had such a close connection to nature that we would never seek to tame it the way the humans do. Instead, we strive only to live in harmony with our surroundings, encouraging the growth of all life.

I have heard the humans no longer honor the old gods who watch over the forests as the Elves still do. As my gaze sweeps beyond the castle to their city of cobbled streets, heavy stone buildings, and fortified walls, it is obvious they have abandoned the old ways long ago.

It is dark outside, but my vision is sharp. Elves can see nearly as well in the night as in the sunlight.

Movement along the far wall of the castle draws my attention.

I turn my head and gape when I catch sight of the princess jumping from her balcony onto a nearby tree and climbing to the ground.

Thick vines cling to the walls beside my balcony, and I test their strength. When I am satisfied that they can bear my weight, I decide to follow her. I'm curious to see where she will go. To the arms of a lover? Or is she attempting to escape our marriage by simply running away?

I scowl as I track her movement along the wall. My nostrils flare as I draw her scent deep into my lungs, committing it to memory so I may use it to follow her. She smells of strawberries and warm summer days—a pleasant combination, and one I will not easily forget.

Moving quickly with the stealth possessed of my people, I surrender to instinct so that I may track her. I will see where she goes, then determine whether I will confront her.

CHAPTER 3

LYANA

I creep as quietly as I can along the garden wall, careful to remain concealed in the shadows. I trace my fingers along the uneven stone to guide my path as I make my way toward the hidden exit.

As soon as my fingers touch the long trailing vines that cover my escape, I carefully part them and slip through the curtain into the forest. The moon is only a quarter full, but it casts enough light that I'm able to navigate the worn path safely through the woods.

Shadows of nocturnal creatures dance at the edge of my vision as I glide along the hard-packed dirt. I am not worried about predators, however. Between my father's guards and the Dwarves who live in the mountains, no wolf or bear would dare hunt in this territory.

A cool breeze whips through the forest. I pull my cloak tighter around me to ward off the chill. I hope Bran is on guard duty this evening, but I cannot be sure. I normally only visit him at the end of the week when I know I will catch him. It's been three days since I saw him last—three days too long.

As I ascend the steep track toward the mountain entrance, I notice a shape moving up ahead. I stop and crouch. I cannot simply show up unannounced. The guards might mistake me for an invader and launch an arrow straight through me.

Bringing my hands to my mouth, I produce the soft bird call that Bran taught me to let the guards know that a friend, not an enemy, approaches.

The shape in the distance stills and sends an answering call, letting me know I may reveal myself without fear of being shot.

I stand and wave into the darkness, knowing the Dwarves have much keener night vision than I do. They can probably see me very clearly, whereas I can only make out the vague shape of a man. At least... I think it's a man. It is hard to distinguish Dwarves at this great distance. They are similar in height to humans. The men and women both have a heavily muscular build, with the same broad shoulders, flat chests, and narrow hips.

The man rushes toward me, and I smile as soon as I recognize Bran. He's only half a head taller than I am, but he is so muscular that when he gathers me into his arms and spins, I feel wrapped in an oversized bear hug.

"What are you doing here, Lyana? How did you know I'd be on guard duty tonight?"

"I didn't." I grin. "I took a chance to come see you."

Even in the dim light of the moon, I read the concern in his features as he studies my face. "Is something wrong?"

My expression falls. Bran has been my best friend since childhood and he knows me too well. Emotions lodge in my throat, and all I can do is nod.

He cups my face with his larger hands, brushing away the

stray tears that escape my lashes with his callused thumbs. "What is it? Tell me, Lyana. Please."

I swallow back a sob. "I am to marry one of the High Elves—Prince Caelen of Rivenyl."

Bran stills, and his lips thin. "No," he whispers. "You cannot marry a High Elf."

CHAPTER 4

CAELEN

I watch in stunned disbelief as the Dwarf gathers her into his arms, hugging her tightly to his chest.

Is this her lover? A Dwarf?

I crouch in the brush and observe from the shadows.

"You cannot marry a High Elf," the Dwarf insists, panic flitting across his features. "They are as cold as they are cruel. How could your father agree to this match?"

How dare he? He acts as though I'm some unscrupulous thief, come to steal the king's daughter.

"He didn't, Bran. He has left the decision up to me. I must marry the prince to ensure peace between our kingdoms and avoid further bloodshed."

"No, you don't!" he snaps. "I will not let you!"

She pushes away from him. "Can't you see? I have no choice."

He clenches his jaw, crossing his arms over his broad chest. "Why did you come here if you're already resigned to your fate?"

"Your people have more dealings with the High Elves than mine do. I want to know more about the blood bond. I've heard only rumors my entire life."

Bran's mouth drifts open as he blinks at her. "He proposed a blood bond with you? Not a simple marriage?"

"What is the difference?" she asks. "I thought they were the same."

He huffs out a breath. "Hardly." Gripping her shoulders, he pulls her close, running a hand over her long black hair. "He probably means to take you during the Wild Hunt as well."

"The Wild Hunt?"

"Aye," he says. "It's a barbaric practice where the male chases the female and claims her roughly beneath the stars during the Hunter's Moon."

I swallow thickly. She does not appear pleased. If she were a High Elf, she would think it an honor that I have offered such a bond, but apparently, humans do not feel the same.

"Stay here, Lyana. You do not have to marry that monster."

"I cannot, Bran. I must marry him for the sake of my subjects. I simply need to know what this prince is like. I've only ever heard dark tales and rumors of the High Elves. They've been our enemies for so long… I had never even seen one up close until today."

I watch as another Dwarf jogs up beside them. Noticing her obvious distress, concern twists his face. "Lyana, what's wrong?"

"She's to be married off to Prince Caelen of Rivenyl, Rob," Bran states flatly.

"No," he breathes, his expression nothing short of devastated. "Not the High Elves."

Her shoulders shake with sobs as Bran runs a hand soothingly down her back.

My upper lip curls into a snarl, my fangs extend into sharpened points, and my deadly claws emerge, aching to rend his flesh from his bones for daring to touch *she* who is to become my mate.

Rob pats her back. "We can hide you, Lyana. Our people will protect you."

"I won't let you do it," Bran states firmly. "You cannot sacrifice yourself in this way."

"I *have* to do this. And yes, I am afraid, but the prince has not threatened me," she says. "I'm simply nervous because I know nothing about him *or* his people beyond the distressing stories I have heard all my life. I did not come here to seek protection. I came because I needed a friend's support."

Friend. I'm surprised at how suddenly my shoulders relax when this word leaves her mouth. I feared he was her lover or secret betrothed. Although, I do not know why it should matter to me. If she were already promised to another, would it not free me of the obligation to marry for peace?

Something inside me, however, realizes a disturbing truth. It matters because, from the moment I first looked upon her, I was enthralled. And I already knew the decision she would make. Determination was written in the tense set of her shoulders, the way she met my gaze, her fisted hands at her sides. She was trying to calm her fears.

This woman has already resolved to bind herself to me for the good of her kingdom. The princess is not the spoiled and pampered human girl I expected. No—she is a selfless leader.

The moment our eyes met, I already considered her mine. Fierce possessiveness rushes through my veins. No mere Dwarf will keep my bride from me.

CHAPTER 5

CAELEN

Bran grasps her small hand in his. "Our people love you, Lyana. I lo—" he stops short and clears his throat before continuing. "There is not a single Dwarf among us who would not lay down their life to protect you."

He cups her face, and rubs his thumb across her cheek. "You alone saved us when no one else cared. Our people would have starved five winters ago if you hadn't convinced your father to aid us."

My brow furrows. *She* is the one who brokered the peace between the Dwarves of the Nylrian Mountains and the Kingdom of Eryadon. My people knew of the treaty, but not what led to its formation.

It seems my future bride is adept at politics. The first thing every great ruler learns is that if you win the hearts of the people, you gain their undying loyalty.

These Dwarves would willingly take up arms simply to keep her from marrying me. That is great power for one person to hold, and I cannot help but be impressed. Dwarves are excellent fighters—the kind that could turn the tide in a war.

I should know. My ancestors manipulated them into waging battle against our enemies, allowing us to conquer great territories for our own kingdom in the process. It is the reason they hate my kind so much now.

"I have to get back to my post," Rob announces. "I'll watch yours as well, Bran."

He hugs the princess before he leaves. I arch a brow as I observe him. These Dwarves make poor sentries for their mountain. Neither man has any idea I am here. If I meant them harm, they would both be dead before they even realized what was happening.

"I'm sorry for coming to you like this. You know how much I hate crying," Lyana admits once Rob is out of earshot.

A faint smile tugs at Bran's lips. "Aye, I do."

"You know you are my closest friend, and I... just needed someone to talk to."

He places two fingers under her chin and tips her face up. "Know that I will always be here for you whenever you need me. If you decide not to marry the elven prince after all, you will always be welcome among my people. We will protect you if your father insists upon anything you do not wish."

"Thank you, Bran, but Father is not forcing me. He would never do that." She pauses. "He left the decision up to me, and I'm doing this for my people. I just... would like to know more about what I'm getting into. You still have not told me about the blood bond. What do you know?"

He frowns. "The High Elves mark their mates as part of the bonding process."

"Mark them?" She blinks. "How?"

He gestures to the curve of her neck. "They have sharp fangs that puncture the artery along the neck. They call it the *dark kiss*. They are savage creatures; they drink their mate's blood."

She swallows rapidly, and places a hand on her throat. "Why would they do that?"

"That, I do not know," he says. "I only know that it's done."

Her brow furrows deeply, and it is easy to see this troubles her.

The act of marking is sacred, *not savage*. And yet, she appears horrified at the mere thought of such a thing.

Bran meets her gaze evenly. "I still don't understand, Lyana. Why are you doing this? Your people already have a treaty with the High Elves."

"If we are going to defeat the Orcs and keep them away from our lands, we have to stop fighting amongst ourselves. Even with the treaty, there are still skirmishes all along the border with Rivenyl. A marriage between our kingdoms could forge a more permanent peace between us."

Bran gives her a pitying look. "You really are set on doing this, aren't you?"

"I have to," she replies solemnly. "What kind of ruler would I be if I were not willing to sacrifice for my people?"

Light peeks over the mountain, promising a new dawn. "I have to go," she mutters. "Father will worry if I'm not home before sunrise."

They stand, and I notice his reluctance to release her. "I beg you to reconsider marrying him, Lyana," he pleads.

She squeezes his hand. "You know I must do this."

His eyes shine with sadness as he watches her walk away. He calls after her, "If you need me, you know where I am."

"Thank you, Bran."

I trail her quietly as she retraces the path back to the castle. When she climbs up the tree to her room, I decide to ascend as well.

This is only supposed to be a political marriage, and nothing more. I do not understand my fascination with the princess, but I cannot stop myself from seeking to learn more about her.

I conceal myself in the shadows of the heavy branches to observe as she putters about her room. Finally, she sits on the edge of her bed. A dozen emotions flit across her face before she drops her head into her hands.

Her shoulders shake with silent sobs, and my heart clenches because I am the cause of her distress. We are enemies, she and I; our people have fought for generations. At this moment, I vow I will prove to her that I will not harm her. I am just as trapped in this situation as she is.

There may be no love between us, but perhaps there can be understanding.

She wipes at her tears, then draws in a deep breath, as if steeling herself for what is to come.

Does she really consider me such a monster?

I must find a way to assuage her fears. It will not do to have my wife and future queen fear me.

When she lifts the hem of her dress to remove it, I quickly avert my gaze. It is not proper to see her bare until after we wed.

The thought occurs to me that it is not strictly proper to spy on her, either.

With a heavy sigh, I climb down the tree as my conscience wins out and I trudge back to my room.

CHAPTER 6

LYANA

I quickly slip into my sleep gown and crawl into bed. Pulling the comforter over my shoulders, I snuggle into the sheets. Since I did not sleep at all last night, I will try to at least rest for a few hours before my family calls for me.

I close my eyes, but sleep eludes me. I cannot stop thinking about Prince Caelen's green eyes baring my soul as he gave me his blade and his vows. My instincts tell me he will not hurt me, but my mind still urges caution.

I've heard far too many terrible stories about the High Elves to discount them all.

Our people have been enemies for so long, it is hard to put aside all the mistrust between us and forget the history of bloody wars we have fought.

A knock at my door draws my attention. "Enter!" I call out.

The door slowly opens to reveal my stepmother and friend, Rina. With her long, blonde hair braided and twisted in an intricate style atop her head, she is so lovely. Her pregnancy lends a healthy glow to her skin. She sits on the edge of the bed and gently strokes my hair, brushing it back from my face.

Her hazel eyes search mine. "I know you wish to do what is best for the kingdom, but I would see you happy, Lyana. Prince Fredrik would be an excellent husband to you. He is handsome—"

A chuckle bursts from me. "You seem so intent on selling me to him, I wonder if you wish him for yourself," I tease.

Her expression falters for a moment before her lips curve up. "Oh, Lyana, do not say such things. You know I only have room for one man in my heart—your father."

With a heavy sigh, I drop back onto the bed and stare wistfully at the ceiling. "I remember well, Rina, how he took you from me." I grin and place a hand on her abdomen. "At least I'll get a sibling out of it."

"Yes, you will." She takes my hand. "I will speak with your father about Fredrik if you wish, my dear."

"No, Father is right. It makes sense for me to marry Prince Caelen. How could I marry Fredrik instead? Knowing that I chose my happiness over the lives of my people?"

Her pursed lips lead me to believe that my answer disturbs her, but I suppose that is because she loves me and wants only the best for my future.

I sit up in bed. "I appreciate you, Rina—really, I do—but I have made up my mind. I suppose all that's left is to inform Father."

She dips her head. "Of course." She squeezes my hand, then stands. "I will see you downstairs."

When I enter the dining room, I find Father and Rina already there. I take the seat beside him, opposite my stepmother, and he turns his gaze to me. "Now that you have had more time to think about it, what have you decided?"

Father has never been one to mince words, so his blunt question does not surprise me. "I will marry Prince Caelen for the good of our kingdom and our people."

A pained smile curls Father's lips as a tear slips down his cheek. "You remind me so much of her. She was selfless like you."

I swallow against the knot in my throat when he brings up my mother. She died giving birth to my younger sister. Neither of them survived.

Rina's gaze drops to her plate. I've often wondered if she ever feels jealous of my father's memories of my mother. She has said nothing, but I still worry for her.

I reach across the table and grip her hand. She lifts her eyes to me and smiles.

"So much of who I am was shaped by you as well, Rina." I glance at my father. "I think Mother would have given you her blessing."

Rina's eyes shine with happiness. "Thank you, Lyana."

Father sighs heavily as he blinks back tears. "After breakfast, I will summon Prince Caelen and his people to the throne room so they may hear your decision."

I nod before turning my attention to my eggs and toast. Suddenly, my appetite has completely vanished and my stomach twists as dread settles deep in my gut.

Today, I make an important commitment for my kingdom's future. I only pray that I choose well for us all.

CHAPTER 7

LYANA

As we wait in the throne room for Prince Caelen, I fidget with the fabric of my skirt and feel faintly nauseous, as my nerves flutter in a state of utter disarray. I peer over at my stepmother, who scowls as she studies my father.

I appreciate how much she cares for me, but deep down, I know that this decision is right. Prince Caelen does, too, or he would not have proposed in the first place. So, I am marginally less afraid than I was yesterday.

When the doors open and he walks in, surrounded by his entourage, I swallow against the knot of worry in my stomach and force my gaze to remain locked on him.

With his dark tunic and pants, he cuts a strong, lean figure. He strides closer, light streaming through the windows gilding his short-cropped hair like spun gold. His face is a perfect, impassive mask as he approaches the throne. He bows to my father, demonstrating respect, and I'm surprised when he turns to me and bows even lower.

His eyes snap up to mine, and I lose myself in their intense, green depths.

This is the man who will be my husband. The face I will learn better than my own. I only pray that our marriage will be blessed with friendship, at least. We already share a common goal—peace. We are both here, forging an agreement not entirely ideal for either of us. That must be a good omen for our future relationship. We will be the kind of rulers who put our kingdom and our people before ourselves.

Prince Caelen straightens. Rather than return his attention to my father to hear our decision, his gaze lingers on me. His expression remains cold, yet his eyes search mine with great anticipation. "I would know your answer to my proposal, Princess Lyana."

"I accept your offer of marriage, Prince Caelen."

He nods once. "If you are amenable, I propose that we wed immediately. We can hold a human ceremony here and an Elven one in my kingdom."

My father leans forward. "Surely, you must realize my daughter needs time to prepare."

"It is all right, Father." I turn to Caelen. "How soon do you suggest?"

"I…" He blinks, and I can tell that I have surprised him. He clears his throat before resuming his unbroken, stoic mask. "Tomorrow."

"Tomorrow?" Rina interrupts, alarm raising the pitch of her voice. "That is not enough time to—"

"It is fine, Rina," I reassure her. I meet Caelen's gaze. "We will wed tomorrow."

Caelen's eyes hold mine for a moment before he bows again. "Tomorrow, then." His guards follow him from the room.

I slump in my chair. Only now does the true impact of my

words hit me. I do not know what compelled me to agree so quickly.

I can hardly believe I'll be wed tomorrow.

Perhaps it is my nature. I've always been one to face any challenge head-on, hating to delay the inevitable.

Father turns to me, his mouth agape. "You are certain you wish to do this so quickly?"

Rina steps over to me and clutches my hand. "You do not have to do this, Lyana. Prince Fredrik—"

"Prince Fredrik may have wealth, and I cannot deny he is handsome, but a marriage to him will not improve the lives of our people as much as one to Prince Caelen will."

Tears brighten her eyes. "Oh, Lyana."

I touch her cheek. "Do not weep for me, Rina. All will be well. The prince's agreement speaks to his character. He is a ruler who places the needs of his people above his own, just as I do. Despite his cold exterior, he must have some sort of heart if he will sacrifice his freedom to secure a lasting treaty."

Father wraps one arm around my shoulder and the other around Rina's waist as he pulls us into a hug. "I will send out the announcements while you"—he gestures to Rina— "help Lyana prepare for her wedding."

Rina sniffs and wipes at her eyes as she nods.

CHAPTER 8

LYANA

I stand in front of the full-length mirror, arms outstretched, as the seamstress takes measurements and adjusts stitches. A faint smile tilts my mouth; I am wearing my mother's wedding gown. I saved it for this day. Little did I know it would come so soon, and not as I'd imagined.

I always thought I'd marry for love, but I suppose marrying for peace is a far more noble endeavor.

Rina's eyes are red rimmed as she appraises me. "You are absolutely lovely, my dear."

"Thank you."

As my dressmaker continues the fitting, the mood is somber. What should be a joyful occasion is mired in sadness. Everyone in this room pities me because my future husband is the High Elf Prince of Rivenyl.

When the seamstress finishes with my dress, she pulls out a swath of sheer fabric. The silver fibers glimmer like starlight as she lifts them against my form to take measurements.

I study the material curiously. "What is this for?"

Her cheeks flush red as her gaze darts to Rina. I notice Rina blushes, too. "Lyana, this is what you will wear after the reception. A gown for the bedchamber to consummate the marriage."

I inhale sharply. "But... this is completely sheer. It—"

"My dear child, do you know what happens between a man and a woman on the night of their wedding?" Rina grimaces as she tenderly brushes a stray lock of hair behind my ear.

"I—I have heard stories," I offer. "I know that a man and woman lie together in the marriage bed, but I must admit... I am not clear on the details of what is expected."

Rina asks the servants to leave the room. As soon as they are gone, she catches my hand in hers. "Let us talk, my darling. I will tell you everything you must know."

CHAPTER 9

CAELEN

As the seamstress holds the sheer fabric out to me for my appraisal, I rub the material between my thumb and forefinger, studying it in confusion. "What is the purpose of this fabric?" I ask. "It does not conceal anything."

Ruvaen's brow is furrowed as well. I am certain my question echoes his thoughts.

The seamstress ducks her head. "It is the covering you will both wear when you are presented to one another on the wedding night." She pauses. "The princess will wait for you in the bedchamber. Several witnesses will be present to make certain the marriage is consummated—"

"Witnesses?" I blurt, completely aghast. "On our wedding night?"

She nods. "It is tradition, my lord."

"Absolutely not. I will not claim my wife in front of a room full of strangers. A wedding night is private, meant only to be shared between the couple." My head whips toward Ruvaen. "I must speak with the king."

Ruvaen's eyes flash with worry. "Perhaps you should reconsider, my prince. This is a human tradition, after all. Do we not expect the princess to honor our Elven bonding traditions when she goes with you to Rivenyl?"

I turn my gaze to the mirror as I consider his words. My cheeks and the tips of my ears are tinged a light green as anger twists my gut. I understand his point, but cannot ignore my instincts. I will not allow strangers to gaze upon my bride's naked body, and I will certainly not have them present for the consummation of our bond. I cannot believe these humans adhere to such a barbaric practice.

Drawing in a deep breath, I realize that Ruvaen is right. I cannot barge into the throne room and start making demands concerning the kingdom's traditions. What I can do, however, is speak with my bride and seek her thoughts on this custom. If she wishes for witnesses to be present, I will comply, but if she feels this must be done for tradition's sake, I will refuse to participate.

As the sun begins to set, I step out onto the balcony and contemplate my future. The end of the day is always a somber, reflective time for me, perhaps because that was the time my brother and I would lounge in the gardens at home and chat.

Dhurvaen had so many plans for his life. He was a noble man and would have made an even greater king. He was strong and brave, one of the fiercest warriors among us. He was always discussing our future and the bright path we would forge for our kingdom. Whereas I always knew that I would be his right hand, his brother, and his counsel.

I direct a heavy sigh at the gardens and the forest beyond the wall. It was a beautiful dream, and I will forever regret it cannot come to pass. He was the better man, and I fear that I may never fill the void left behind by his passing.

Footsteps behind me draw my attention. Without turning, I recognize Ruvaen by the cadence of his tread along the stone balcony. "Are you well, my prince?"

With another sigh, I nod. "As well as I can be, Ruvaen." I turn to him. "I feel as if I am doing what Dhurvaen would have done, but I cannot be certain if it is the right course for our people."

He cocks his head to the side. "You make a sacrifice for your kingdom—a selfless one, my prince. One that I am not sure even your brother would have made." He arches a brow. "You know how he felt about humans."

A grin twists my lips. He is right, I suppose. Dhurvaen would not have agreed to marry a human—even for the good of our people.

I nod in agreement. "He has not even been gone a year. Sometimes, I believe I remember him through a lens of my own making."

Ruvaen rests a hand on my shoulder. "I think everyone does when they lose someone, Caelen."

He is free to use my given name. Ruvaen practically raised the three of us—my brother, my younger sister, Nurala, and me. He was our mentor and guardian since we were children.

"Our parents were wise to choose you as our teacher, Ruvaen."

He inclines his head. "I feel blessed to have had a hand in your education. All three of you grew into leaders anyone would be willing to follow."

Heaving a sigh, I lower my gaze. "The people wanted Dhurvaen. I am a poor substitute."

"Do not be so hard on yourself, Caelen. You are a good man." He gestures to the castle around us. "You have already chosen a path of sacrifice for the welfare of your people." He gives me a hesitant look. "There is something I must say to you."

Something about his tone concerns me. "What is it?"

"I worry that you compare yourself too often to your brother. That you try to live up to a standard you believe he would have set. But the two of you were always so very different, Caelen. Your brother's kingdom would have been one of war, but yours will be one of peace. Both approaches make for a strong kingdom, but only one has the potential to spare countless lives." He pauses. "I cared for your brother as if he were my own child, just as I do you and your sister. I miss him every day. But I beg you... do not try to be who you suppose he would have been. You will be a great ruler. Of this, I have no doubt."

His words touch me. Deeply. I swallow against the lump in my throat. "Thank you, Ruvaen."

He dips his chin in a subtle nod. "I am off to bed. We have a long, important day ahead of us, my prince."

My expression falls at the reminder, as the image of Lyana crying last night fills my mind. I must find a way to show her that she need never fear me.

"Yes, we do."

After Ruvaen leaves, I turn my attention back to the gardens. Movement in the shadows below catches my eye. I recognize Prince Fredrik immediately but am surprised to see the queen approach him.

His family rules the neighboring kingdom of Winterhold. I suppose it is only natural he would have come to present himself for the princess's hand to forge an alliance between their kingdoms.

I do not understand, however, why he is alone with the queen right now.

He drops to one knee and takes the queen's hand in his, pressing a kiss to the back of her knuckles before rising again. I train my ears toward them, eavesdropping.

"What must I do to convince her to choose me?" he asks. "You were so certain that the princess would accept me, but you were wrong."

"I did not anticipate the Prince of Rivenyl would offer his hand."

Fredrik shakes his head. "But surely marriage to me would be better for the kingdom. Eryadon could use our strength to fight the High Elves and protect your borders."

"I already tried to persuade her and the king," she replies. "It was of no use. But perhaps we could alter our strategy."

"What would you suggest?"

Deafening thunder booms overhead before she can answer.

The wind begins to howl around the castle, and the air is heavy with moisture, promising rain. I lift my gaze to the sky and the dark clouds roiling above. Lightning arcs through the clouds in a brilliant display.

I do not know if the old gods still linger in these lands, but I will take the impending storm as a sign of their blessing. Showers on the day of bonding are the gods raining down their blessings from above.

When I scan the gardens again, the queen and Prince Fredrik are gone. The humans do not realize how sharp Elvish hearing is. I overheard the queen trying to pressure the princess and the king into accepting Fredrik's hand when we first arrived.

It seems the queen has not given up on this idea just yet, despite our impending ceremony. Now, I find myself wondering if there will still be a wedding tomorrow.

CHAPTER 10

LYANA

When morning comes, I step onto the balcony and peer at the dark clouds overhead. The fresh scent of rain lingers in the air as rolling thunder rumbles above us. Lightning streaks across the sky, and heavy drops begin to fall.

What an ominous backdrop for my wedding day. We've had nothing but clear skies the past few weeks, yet today of all days, a storm brews. Maybe this is a sign that I'm making a mistake.

I've always heard that rain is a terrible omen on one's wedding day.

A knock at the door startles me, and I turn to find Rina and a servant entering. Rina's eyes are glassy as she presents my dress to me. More servants enter while she guides me toward the full-length mirror with a pained smile. "We have much to do, my dear. Are you sure this is what you want?"

I take her hand and squeeze gently. "It may not be what I want, but I know in my heart that it is right."

A tear drips from her lashes and rolls down her cheek. She quickly brushes it away and forces a bright smile to her face.

"All right." She turns me to face the mirror. "You will be the most beautiful bride there ever was."

With Rina's help, it takes far less time to get ready than I thought it would. As I stand before the mirror in my wedding gown, a faint smile tugs my lips. I wish my mother were here to see me wearing her dress. I can only imagine how happy she must have been when she wore it the day she married my father.

As if my very thoughts have summoned him, he enters the room.

He smiles warmly and pulls me into an embrace. "You are just as lovely as your mother."

His words strike a chord deep inside me. "Thank you, Father," I barely manage as I blink back tears.

Father tips up my chin. "You are sure this is what you want to do?"

I nod. "You know it is right, Father."

"Aye. I do." He sighs. "The Dwarves do not believe so, however. They've come for the wedding, their king demanding that I send your future husband fleeing to the hills rather than allow him to marry you."

I chuckle. "They are honorable people. They simply worry for me."

"Especially Bran," Father adds. "We'll have to keep a close eye on him at the reception or I suspect your new husband will be the proud owner of a black eye this evening for stealing his best friend."

A faint smile crests my lips because I know he's right.

Father offers me his arm. "All right, my darling daughter. Are you ready?"

I loop my arm through his. "Yes, I am."

When we reach the great hall, Father pauses just outside the doors. My heart hammers, knowing that my future husband is waiting for me on the other side. Drawing in a deep, steadying breath, we start forward.

The guards throw open the doors, and my gaze flies to Prince Caelen standing at the end of the aisle with another Elf at his side. His eyes snap up to meet mine, and I can barely breathe.

Dressed in flowing, elegant robes of emerald, he stands regal and handsome. His outfit perfectly complements his eyes and flawless skin, lending an ethereal yet fierce beauty to his features.

Beautiful silk ribbons adorn the Great Hall. Sunlight filters in through the stained-glass windows. Their patterns and colors a stark contrast to the gray stone of the castle, and the bouquets of white roses at the ends of each aisle. Scattered white rose petals line the carpeted walkway to the altar, filling the air with their sweet perfume.

As Father and I start down the aisle, I pray to the gods and the spirit of my mother to grant me the strength and courage to see this through. Today, my former enemy will become my husband and lover.

CHAPTER 11

CAELEN

R uvaen flanks me at the front of the great hall as I await my bride. The humans in the crowd study us with a mixture of fascination and displeasure. I am sure many would prefer the princess marry anyone but me.

I contemplate the Dwarves. Many eye me with suspicion and outright anger—especially her friend, Bran. I train my face into an impassive mask and hold my head high.

Scanning the great hall as we wait for my princess, I note the decorations. The crowd is seated on rows of wooden benches with an aisle straight through the middle. Flowers adorn the ends and rose petals line the carpeted walkway.

The many stained-glass windows arrayed in the walls cast sparkling reflections on the polished stone floors. The doors open, and my eyes snap to Lyana.

I drag in a deep breath. She is dressed in a long, flowing white gown embroidered with silver threads in an intricate pattern of roses and vines. A crown of silver adorns her head.

Her long black hair is arranged on her head like a second braided crown, revealing the elegant column of her neck.

She walks down the aisle with her father. When they reach the dais, he takes her hand and places it in my own. His gaze falls hard upon me in unspoken warning, and I nod, hoping he knows that I will never harm his daughter.

Her dainty hand is warm in mine, and her skin is petal soft. The top of her head barely reaches my chin. She lifts her face to me and her golden-brown eyes fix upon my own as if searching for something, but I do not know what. Gently, she takes my other hand and I note their trembling as they rest in mine.

The priest before us instructs her to recite a set of vows. Her gaze holds my own as she vows to love, honor, and cherish me.

Love. I did not think she would promise this to me, but she does. Suddenly, I have no hesitation promising the same when it is my turn to recite the vows in return.

My heart is lighter just knowing that she would offer such a beautiful gift so readily to me—a perfect stranger and her former enemy. It gives me hope that perhaps ours will be as much a marriage for love as for the securing of a treaty.

A faint smile tilts my lips as I study her—my human mate and bride.

Her father instructs that I must now kiss her to signal the end of the ceremony. Awkwardly, she stretches onto her toes, and I lean forward just enough to press my lips to hers in a chaste kiss.

When she pulls away, I instinctively run my tongue over my bottom lip, tasting the delicate flavor of her kiss.

Together, we turn to face the crowd and walk down the aisle into the great dining hall. I am unsure of what to expect, so I follow her lead as she guides me to a long table near the front.

We take the seats directly at its center as the guests file in behind us. Lengthy rows of tables extend around us, covered in fine silverware and goblets. Servants appear, bearing trays overflowing with cooked meats, fruits, vegetables, and bread.

More servants fill our goblets with fermented ale, and I perceive the Dwarves partaking more than they probably should, judging by their boisterous behavior which grows louder with each drink.

Lyana and I sit side by side in silence. To my left, Ruvaen leans in and whispers, "You should at least try to speak with her. It will make things less awkward for you this evening."

My cheeks and the tips of my ears flush with warmth as I realize he is referring to the consummation of our marriage.

I consider what I might say to my bride as I drink from my glass, the bitter liquid rolling across my tongue. I set my goblet down and turn to face her, watching her down one glass, then another. Suddenly her intent dawns on me; she hopes to dull her nerves for what comes later.

"Lyana."

She turns toward me just as the first musical notes fill the air. "We are supposed to dance the opening dance," she says. "It is tradition."

Tradition. I ponder this word, remembering what other traditions concern tonight. The thought tastes like bitter acid on my tongue as I recall the supposed witnesses to our joining. She stands, and I offer her my arm as we walk to the center of the room.

The guests fall silent, their gazes heavy on us. I may not know much about humans and their traditions, but I do know how to dance. My people love to dance, and music is a source of great enjoyment among us.

I turn to the musicians. "Do you know *volkaera?*"

One nods. "Yes."

"Will you please play it?"

I face Lyana as the slow, hauntingly beautiful melody begins. I chose this specifically because it is a dance of intrigue. The steps placing us so close together we may speak quietly to one another without being overheard.

I raise my palm, and she places her hand against mine as we circle one another. The tempo changes, and we turn, circling in the opposite direction. Her golden-brown eyes are locked on mine as we fall into rhythm, our palms hovering close yet not quite touching in a dance of give and take. The room falls away until we are the only ones here. My heart pounds as she glides past me and places her palm against mine once more.

This is an ancient dance—older than the conflict between our kingdoms. It was once performed by High Elven lords who came to the human kingdom in search of wives. Long before we were enemies, before the great and devastating war that divided us.

The tempo changes, and I wrap my hands around her waist, lifting her in a quick spin before setting her feet back on the ground. I'm surprised by how little she weighs compared to one of my people. When I gather her close to my chest, I can feel the pounding of her heart beneath her breast. My nostrils flare as I drink in her delicate scent, a heady bouquet.

We dance and whirl across the room in a series of intricate steps. Our movements are smooth and fluid as we weave around each other, and I cannot help but hope this is a sign of what our union may be.

She places her palm in mine again as we circle one another, and I dare to cautiously thread my fingers through hers, watching in wonder as her cheeks flare a lovely shade of pink. My people are taught from a very young age to hide our emotions behind impassive masks. I am completely captivated as my gaze holds hers and a dozen emotions flicker across her face. I stare unabashedly as I study her, completely and utterly enthralled.

The music ends far too soon, and I blink as I return to my senses. Couples join us on the floor as a joyful tune begins to play. Bran approaches my bride and taps on her shoulder. She turns to him, flashing a dazzling smile that rivals the brightness of the sun.

Irrational jealousy steals through me. I wish she greeted me as kindly as she does him. I narrow my eyes as Bran sweeps into a bow and extends his hand, whisking her away from me to whirl about the room.

How dare this Dwarf take my bride? I level an icy glare and stalk toward him but stop when I catch sight of her face. She shows more joy at this moment than anytime she has looked at me. I blink slowly, reconsidering.

Challenging him is not the way to win Lyana's favor. No. That is what Bran wants, and I refuse. I understand the game he tries to play as he smirks in my direction.

Instead, I approach them calmly, though I am anything but. I extend my hand, and she cautiously takes it. I pull her away, and we whirl around the room, rejoining the other dancing couples.

She tilts her head to the side. "I did not think the High Elves liked to dance."

I arch a brow. "It seems there are a great many things we do not know about one another."

"I suppose you are right," she replies, her expression unreadable.

When the reception ends, a group of servants guides us from the dining hall to the far wing of the castle. It seems we will not be sleeping in either of our rooms as I assumed.

This part of the castle appears deserted but it is still neat and clean, as if ready for guests at all times. I'm ushered into one room and watch her disappear into the next.

I do not understand why we have been separated until a servant steps forward and begins unfastening my robe. I pull away.

"I can do this myself," I insist. "Simply tell me where to go once I am changed."

Her eyes widen slightly before she nods and gestures to the sheer fabric on the bed. "Once you have changed into your joining robes, go through those doors. The princess will be waiting on the other side."

Clamoring in the hallway draws my attention, and I frown. "What is that noise?"

"The witnesses, my lord."

This is the moment I have been dreading. I push past her and fling open the door. I step into the hallway and face the bustling group, blocking the doorway that leads to my bride. "Stop," I state firmly. "You will not come any closer."

A man with gray hair and elegant dress, suggesting he is someone of importance, glares at me. "We are the witnesses. This is tradition. How dare you—"

"No," I spit through gritted teeth. "How dare you presume this is what my bride wishes?"

They blink at me, and I realize I have caught their attention.

"I will honor this tradition, but only if she agrees. If she does not, none of you may enter. If anyone dares enter without our express permission, you'll meet the end of my blade," I growl. "Do you understand?"

Without waiting for a response, I turn on my heel and head back into my bedroom.

"You may all leave. I must prepare for my bride," I tell the servants. They bow low, then rush to exit.

I remove my clothing and pull on the sheer fabric covering. I glance down at my body, wondering if she will find me strange. I've heard our anatomy is remarkably similar to Terran males, but I do not know if it is truth.

It is customary to give a gift to our bonded one on the night of first joining. I take the small wooden box from the pocket of my discarded tunic, hoping she will be pleased with this token. I hold it tightly as I move to the door between our rooms and gently knock.

"You may enter," she calls.

Cautiously, I push the door open and step into pitch-black darkness.

My eyes readily adjust to the absence of light. I thought humans lacked night vision, but perhaps I was wrong.

Lyana's black hair hangs loosely around her shoulders in long, silken waves. I study the lovely contours of her face, marveling at her delicate cheeks, nose, and brow.

I allow my gaze to travel over her body. The sheer fabric does nothing to conceal her form from me. My eyes move down the elegant column of her neck to the soft swell of her breasts, the slight dip of her waist, and the gentle flare of her hips. Desire rises within me as I drink in her exquisite, graceful form. She is more beautiful than I ever imagined.

"I hope you'll forgive the darkness, my lord," she says. "It is tradition for there to be witnesses to our… joining. I thought it might provide us more privacy." Cautiously, she extends her arm toward me. "If you follow the sound of my voice, you will find me."

I tilt my head to the side. She does not realize I can see her in the darkness without difficulty.

CHAPTER 12

LYANA

"I can see perfectly well in the darkness, Princess."

"Oh." I wince as my face grows hot. "I did not realize, my lord."

"Please," he says. "Call me Caelen."

"Caelen," I repeat his name softly.

My trembling arm is still extended out before me. I move to retract it, but his warm hand finds mine and squeezes gently. His skin is callused against my own, but this is natural, I would think, for a skilled swordsman. "I have asked the witnesses to remain outside. They will not enter without your permission. I understand they are part of your tradition, but I would know your thoughts before I allow them to be present for our first joining."

Our first joining. I swallow against the knot of worry in my stomach as I consider his words.

Despite my nerves, a measure of relief flows over me at the thought that we will not have witnesses. "I do not want them here."

"As you wish, my bride."

He releases my hand, and his steps reverberate softly as he pads across the room to the door. "There will be no witnesses to our joining. You may all leave now," he commands.

A rumble of voices in the hallway tells me that many are upset by this decision, but I care not. I have never approved of this tradition and am glad that we will not be honoring it.

His hand takes mine again, and although I cannot see him, I tip up my chin and give him a tremulous smile. "Thank you, Caelen. Please, call me Lyana."

"Lyana," he repeats my name like a gentle caress.

He moves closer. Heat radiates from his body, and my every nerve ending hums in awareness of him. The smell of warm cinnamon fills my nostrils as I breathe in his scent.

He brushes the hair from my face and lightly runs the pad of his thumb over my cheek. I draw in a shaking breath as my body trembles with nervous anticipation.

He lifts my hand and presses a tender kiss to the top of my knuckles. "You do not need to fear me, Lyana."

"I… do not," I offer a half truth. "I'm merely nervous."

It's more than nerves. I've heard the first time can be very painful and I do not know how High Elf men compare to humans. I only know that he's much taller than most human men. What if we do not fit?

"I must ask," he murmurs, his voice low and smooth like velvet. "What is the purpose of the witnesses?"

"To ensure that our marriage is properly consummated, my lord."

He's silent for so long, I would think he is not even still here if not for his hand in mine. Finally, he speaks. "I do not understand. How does one *properly* consummate a marriage?"

Warmth rushes to my cheeks. "The sheets. They... are inspected after we—"

"Inspected?" he asks incredulously. "For what?"

I swallow hard. "Blood."

"Blood?" he asks, confusion in his tone.

I did not think it possible for my face to heat even more, but now it feels as if it's on fire. "The blood of my maidenhead. It should stain the sheets after a woman's barrier is breached for the first time."

He inhales sharply. "Human females bleed when they join?"

"Yes, but only the first time."

"Is this... painful?" he asks, a note of worry in his voice.

"I've heard it can be."

"I... still do not understand. Why is it important for others to see this blood upon the sheets after our first joining?"

"I understand that there are two reasons, my lord," I reply, struggling to keep my voice even. "The first is to prove that I came to our marriage bed a virgin. The second is so that none can question the validity of our union; so that it cannot be annulled later. Do your people not practice something similar?"

"No, we do not." He pauses. "We do not have to join until you are ready. We can wait."

"But what about the sheets? Even if they are not here as witnesses, someone will still inspect them. It is tradition and—"

"I will send for one of my men to discreetly bring us blood from a chicken or some such. Would that suffice?"

A smile lifts my lips. "Yes." My shoulders relax as the tension drains from my body. "Thank you." I grope for the robe that should be close to the bed. It's so dark in here, I cannot see.

"Here," Caelen says, and I feel the press of fabric in my hand. "Were you searching for this?"

I nod and quickly slip the robe over my shoulders, tying the sash around my waist.

I hear the soft rustle of clothing and wonder if he is dressing as well.

His footsteps cross the room toward the window, and he flings the curtains wide, allowing silver moonlight to spill into the room. Soft knit pants hug lean hips and toned thighs, but he wears nothing else.

The soft light illuminates his broad shoulders and muscular physique. He moves with the same fluid and lethal grace as he did when we were dancing. The glimmering beams accentuate the sharp lines of his face and the pointed tips of his ears as he turns to me.

As my gaze travels down his form, I'm drawn to something in his hand. A square, wooden object, but I'm uncertain what it is.

He holds it out and I cautiously take it. "What is this?"

"My people traditionally present our bonded one with a gift on the first night of marriage."

I study the box. The top is carved in intricate scrolling patterns of vines with heart-shaped leaves. It's like a work of art unto itself. I find a small latch on the side and when I release it, the most beautiful ring I've ever beheld nestles inside.

The glow from the window highlights a delicate silver band shaped like tiny vines with miniscule leaves. In the center, a small round stone shimmers like moonlight. It's nothing short of breathtaking. "This is beautiful," I whisper.

"It has been in our family for many generations."

"I—" I stop short, uncertain what to say, before finally deciding upon. "This is too much, Caelen. I—I did not even get you anything."

Carefully, he removes the ring from the box and slips it onto my finger. "It was my mother's," he says, his voice thick with emotion. "It looks lovely on you."

I lift my gaze to his. "Thank you."

I place the box on the side table, next to the blade he offered me when he proposed.

"Come," he says. "Let us sleep."

He carefully tugs on my hand, guiding me to the bed. I slip beneath the covers, lying on my side. When I feel the bed dip behind me, I gasp, and he stills.

"Do you wish me to sleep on the floor?" he asks. His tone is nothing but sincere, making me regret my reaction.

"No," I reply as I scoot to the opposite edge. I grab two pillows and place them between us as a barrier, hoping to avoid any awkwardness as we sleep.

A long sigh escapes him. He is probably just as exhausted as I am after today.

"So… what will happen when we reach your kingdom?" I ask, curious to know what awaits me. I shudder inwardly as I think of what Bran mentioned about the Wild Hunt.

"My father will host a feast and—"

A soft knock at the door draws our attention.

"Who is there?" Caelen asks, sitting up in the bed.

"It's me, Ruvaen, my prince."

"Ruvaen?"

Caelen turns to me. "Forgive me. I will see what he wants and send him away quickly."

I sit up, wrapping the blankets around me as Caelen opens the door just enough to speak through it. "Is something wrong?"

"My lord, I—" he starts but stops.

"What is it?" Caelen presses.

"I overheard some of the humans say that you had refused the traditional consummation witnessing. They said they believed you may be having... difficulties," he says a bit hesitantly.

"Difficulties?" Caelen asks.

"It is not uncommon to have anxiety before the first joining, my prince. I could give you a potion that would help."

"I do not need any potion, Ruvaen," Caelen practically growls. "My mate did not wish to participate in this barbaric tradition, so I sent the witnesses away."

Mate. The term surprises me, but I suppose this is how the Elves refer to their wives.

He continues. "I do need you to bring me some chicken blood first thing in the morning, however."

"Chicken... blood?"

"Discreetly," Caelen adds.

"Of—of course, my prince."

Ruvaen's eyes dart briefly to mine before he quickly lowers his gaze. "Forgive me, my lady."

"It's all right," I reply.

Color rises in his cheeks and he bows low. "I will take my leave of you both. Please, excuse my intrusion."

Caelen claps a hand on his shoulder. "All is well, Ruvaen. I will speak to you in the morning."

When he leaves, Caelen returns to the bed. He sits beside me. "You'll have to excuse Ruvaen. He means well. He is my mentor. He was the one who taught my siblings and me when we were growing up." A light chuckle escapes him, and I realize it's the closest thing I've heard to a laugh out of his mouth since we met. "Dhurvaen was always giving him trouble. He used to play pranks on him all the time."

Sadness flits briefly across his face, and my heart hurts for his loss. "I was sorry to hear about your brother."

His eyes snap up to mine. Our people have been enemies for a long time, and he probably doubts the sincerity of my words.

"I know what it is to lose an older brother," I add. "But mine was to sickness, not battle."

He nods slowly. "I remember hearing of his passing. Prince Arthur was known as a fierce warrior, even among my own people."

"Yes, he was." A wistful smile crests my lips at the memory of my brother. "He would have been a great king."

Caelen lies back on the bed, staring up at the ceiling with a faraway look. "I believe Dhurvaen would have been as well."

Silence settles in the space between us. It seems my new husband and I have more in common than I realized. Neither of us were supposed to rule, and yet, here we are: each of us heir to a kingdom at the price of losing a beloved sibling.

We lie side by side in the darkness. Perhaps he is not the monster I feared him to be. His actions this evening have certainly shown him to be a man of honor.

After a moment, he whispers. "Goodnight, Lyana."

"Goodnight, Caelen."

CHAPTER 13

CAELEN

M ovement startles me awake, and my eyes snap open to find Lyana asleep on her back. Silver moonlight filters in through the curtains, casting her body in a pale glow.

Her long black hair spreads beneath her on the pillow. Dark lashes fan over pink cheeks, and her lips are open in a small O.

I prop my weight on my elbow as I study her, relaxed in sleep. Her gently rounded ears where an Elf's would be pointed, lovely, smooth skin, and full, perfect pink lips. She is enchanting, my bride, and I am completely mesmerized.

She shivers, and I carefully pull the comforter over her shoulders, tucking her into their warmth before rolling onto my back. I stare at the ceiling. I can hardly believe I am married. Although I have not bound her to me in the ways of my people, I already feel protective of her, possessive even.

She vowed to love, honor, and cherish me when she

spoke her human vows of bonding, and I am deeply moved by this.

A muffled scream in the hallway abruptly cuts short, and I freeze. The heavy sound of booted steps echoes outside the door. I slip from the bed and creep toward it.

I glance over my shoulder at Lyana, but she does not stir. Perhaps her human ears are not as keen as mine.

I stop beside the door, my sharp fangs and claws descending as I ready to defend us against whatever lurks in the hallway.

A deafening *boom* sounds, and the wooden door flies inward. A man wearing the tabard of Prince Fredrik's house rushes inside. Lyana jerks upright in bed, her gaze wild and unfocused as light floods the room.

The soldier doesn't even take two steps toward the bed before I slash with my claws, ripping his throat out. Red sprays from his wound as he drops to his knees and crumples to the floor in a pool of blood.

Lyana's frantic eyes meet mine. I can only imagine the monster I must appear to her. "What's going on? Who was—"

"One of Prince Fredrik's guards." A snarl rumbles in my chest as I study his lifeless form. "We must find your parents and my people. Hurry. Get dressed."

She nods, and we retrieve our clothing. We face opposite walls as we dress. There is no time for awkwardness between us.

I grab the blade from the side table and place it in her hand as I meet her gaze evenly. "Do not hesitate to use this. Do you understand?"

She nods, and I take her other hand in mine. "Let's go."

CHAPTER 14

LYANA

I t's still night outside as we race through the castle to
my father and Rina's chambers. My heart thunders in
my chest and I pray we reach them in time.

The torches that normally light the hallways are dark.
Caelen clasps my hand firmly, guiding me down the nearly
pitch-black corridors as I tell him how many turns and doors
until we reach our destination.

Light shines dimly up ahead, casting just enough illumination that I no longer fear tripping over my own feet as we
rush to my family.

A soldier wearing Prince Fredrik's colors rushes toward
us. Caelen shoves me behind him, barely avoiding the edge of
the man's blade as he attacks.

Caelen roars and charges forward, twisting to avoid
another swing of the sword as he barrels into the man, slamming him back against the stone wall.

Lightning fast, he rips the soldier apart with his claws.
His lips peel back in a feral snarl as he bares his fangs,

rending flesh from bone. I watch as the man collapses to the floor, blood pumping.

Caelen takes the soldier's sword and then grabs my hand, towing me behind him as we rush down the hallway.

We find an Elf on the floor, his back propped against the wall, and his body surrounded with obsidian blood.

Caelen drops to his knees with a gasp, clutching the man's hand in his. "Ruvaen. What happened?"

"Caelen," he rasps. "Prince Fredrik and his men... they did this. Get the princess to safety. You must hide. You must go."

"I will not leave you."

Caelen helps him up, and I notice the dark blood that covers his clothing as he sags against the wall. "I am injured. I will only slow you down. I do not have much strength left. You have to leave me."

"No."

A shout rings out nearby, and Caelen's head snaps toward it.

"Go!" Ruvaen shouts. "Now! I'll hold them off as long as I can." With a battle cry, he rushes down the hallway to intercept one of Fredrik's soldiers.

Caelen grips my hand. "Where are your parents' chambers?"

"Down there." I point down a long hallway. "We have to hurry, Caelen. Please."

When we reach the doors to my father's chambers, he pushes them open, and we rush inside. "King Gareth!"

My heart stops as I take in the scene before me. Prince Fredrik stands over the still form of my father, crimson blood dripping from his sword.

"No!" An agonized wail rips from my throat.

His head snaps up, eyes feral and glowing yellow now instead of gray. With teeth bared in a snarl, it is easy to see the terrifying wolf within. The muscles of his arms rippling beneath his skin as if readying to fully shift into *wolven* form.

My heart stops with desperate fear for Rina. My eyes dart around the room, searching for her even as Fredrik stalks toward me like a predator closing in on its prey.

"Out of the way, Elf Prince. This is nothing to do with you. The princess must die."

Panic tightens my chest as Fredrik's feral gaze holds mine.

Caelen grips my forearm, pulling me behind him. "She is my mate." A growl rumbles in his chest as he bares his fangs, and deadly claws slide from his fingertips. "You *will not* touch her."

Lightning fast, Caelen rushes Fredrik. They clash in a flurry of fangs and claws and fall to the floor in a tangled mess of limbs, ripping into each other's flesh with savage brutality.

A high-pitched, animalistic yelp rips from Fredrik's throat as Caelen stabs his claws deep into his side. He throws Fredrik back, slamming him against the wall with a sickening *crack*.

Fredrik crumples to the floor in a broken heap, panting heavily as Caelen advances.

The doors burst open behind us. A dozen guards rush into the room—all dressed in the yellow coat of arms of Fredrik's house.

Caelen's arms whip out and wrap solidly around my torso. He pulls me tightly against his chest as he rushes to the balcony. "Hold on to me!"

Instinctively, I wrap my limbs around him as he vaults over the balcony railing and grips the thick, heavy vines that trail down to the gardens below. He descends with dizzying speed. Once we reach the earth, the pounding of dozens of booted feet rends the air.

"Follow me!" I take his hand and guide him toward my secret escape in the garden wall.

To my surprise, he takes the lead, dragging me instead. We're not quite there when arrows begin to rain down all around us, and panic grips me in an iron vise when I notice a boulder blocking the exit.

I turn to Caelen. "How did they know where—"

My eyes fly wide. I track an arrow heading straight for him. "Caelen, look out!"

He turns, but not fast enough. Without hesitation, I throw myself against his chest, knocking him out of its path.

Sharp pain explodes across my side as the arrow sinks deep into my flesh.

Lightning fast, Caelen snaps off the feathered end. He gathers me in one arm and scales the wall with the other. My eyelids flutter as I struggle to stay conscious despite my agonizing pain.

"Rina," I gasp. "We cannot leave her."

He says nothing as he jumps over the wall. We hit the ground hard, and a wail bursts from my throat when the impact jostles the wound in my side.

Caelen wraps both arms around me, tucking me into his chest as he races through the forest at blinding speed.

When we're far enough away, he skids to a halt and drops to his knees. Groggily, I recognize where we are. The Dwarves' mountain stands proudly over Caelen's shoulder. Gripping my face, his panicked green eyes search mine. "Lyana, you must stay awake."

The light of the sunrise filters through the forest, casting just enough illumination that I can see the obsidian blood covering him. My mind floats in a fog-filled haze as darkness dances at the edge of my vision. I reach up and touch his chest where claws have slashed through his tunic and skin. "You're hurt," I barely manage.

"I am fine," he says quickly. "Lyana, the Dwarves. Where is the entrance to their mountain?"

Sleep beckons. It is difficult to talk, but I force the words past my lips. "I cannot find it without Bran's help."

Caelen lifts his head and makes the bird call the Dwarves taught me to let them know a friend has arrived.

A trilling call returns a moment later, followed quickly by an arrow whizzing past Caelen's head. "Stay where you are, Elf," a menacing voice commands. "The next one will go right between your eyes. What are—" He inhales sharply. "Lyana!"

"The princess! Save the princess!" Voices ring out, but I cannot focus long enough to identify them.

Caelen presses a hand to my side, and I peer down to see the deep-red blood pooling around my injury and blooming across the fabric of my dress. "So much blood," I barely manage.

I watch in horror as Caelen extends his fangs and bites into his wrist. He pushes the dripping wound to my mouth. "Drink."

"No." My lips curl in disgust. "I—"

He presses his wrist to my mouth, and I'm too weak to pull away. The bitter taste of blood touches my tongue before he lifts his arm away.

A *thud* sounds beside me, and I lift my eyes to find Bran staring at me, frantic and out of breath. "Lyana!"

Unable to fight the darkness beckoning me, I close my eyes and fall into the void.

CHAPTER 15

LYANA

As awareness returns, shouts cut through the air. I recognize Bran's voice immediately, followed by the low grumble of Caelen's. My brain struggles to process what they're saying.

Gentle hands touch my side, and my eyes snap open to find a Dwarf leaning over me. She flashes a warm smile. "There you are, dear. I knew you'd come back to us."

"Lyana?" Bran rushes to me. He takes my hand and presses a peck to my knuckles. "Oh, gods. What happened? Tell us."

Caelen moves to my other side, his green eyes scanning me. "How do you feel?"

"I—"

"Get back, you villain!" Bran snaps at him. "You're lucky I haven't lopped your head off with my axe yet!"

"Bran," I interject. "He saved me."

All the anger drains from his features, replaced by a stunned expression. "What?"

A tear escapes my lashes. "Father is dead. And Rina... I don't know what they did to her."

"The king is dead?" I recognize the voice of Bran's father —the king of the mountain. "How?"

"Wolf shifters," Caelen answers. "Prince Fredrik's soldiers."

King Edwyrd glares at him. "I wasn't asking *you*, Elf."

"Caelen saved me." My voice comes out a harsh croak. "If not for him, I'd be dead."

King Edwyrd's gaze travels down my form to my bandaged injury. "It certainly doesn't look that way." His face reddens as he turns to Caelen. "Where are your wounds, Elf?"

I blink, finally studying Caelen more closely. Despite his torn tunic and the blood staining his body, he doesn't appear to have a single scratch on him.

"My people heal quickly. You know this, Dwarf King," he says, bitterness tinging his tone.

The king scoffs and turns his attention to me. "Tell me what happened, Princess."

I swallow back a sob as I recall my father's still form. "Prince Fredrik. He killed my father, and his forces captured the castle. We didn't see Rina. I do not know what they did to her."

The king takes my hand and pats it gently. "You're safe with us, Lyana. We'll watch over you and send someone to the castle to find out what happened to your stepmother."

"We cannot stay here." Caelen's voice is steely as he confronts the king. "They will come for us soon."

"Let them!" Bran snaps. "We'll fight—"

"I need to get to Rivenyl." Caelen cuts him off. "I will gather our armies."

"How do we know you are not behind this?" King

Edwyrd demands. "You could be in league with Fredrik—the perfect excuse to bring your armies to our lands."

Bran levels a murderous glare at Caelen. "I say we lock him up in the dungeons, just to be sure."

King Edwyrd looks to his guards. "Take the Elf to—"

He stops abruptly when I reach up and wrap my hand weakly around his forearm. "There is no need to imprison my husband. If Caelen was working with Fredrik, it would have been easier for him to leave me to die. Instead, he brought me here."

"You say *husband*," Bran counters, "but I say *scoundrel*." Clenching his jaw, he narrows his eyes at Caelen. "How did you know the secret call?"

Caelen stills.

"Tell me, Elf."

Caelen lowers his eyes, something akin to guilt flashing across his expression. "I followed Lyana here two nights before our wedding." My mouth drops open. That's how he knew where the hole in the palace garden wall should have been.

Bran narrows his eyes. "You were spying on her?"

"I—" Caelen starts, but I raise my hands in silent bid to allow me to speak.

We do not have time to be standing around arguing.

"Rina is still at the castle." I look to King Edwyrd. "I need to go back and—"

"You're still recovering," Bran says, "You shouldn't be going anywhere."

I open my mouth to protest, but Caelen steps forward.

"I know my way back to the castle. I will search for the queen and find out whether she still lives."

Bran snarls. "Or you plan to return and take over. Your coup successful, the king out of the way, and—"

"Bran, stop," I tell him. "If he wanted that, he could have killed me already."

Bran frowns, considering. "I'll go with you," he concludes.

"It's too dangerous. You'll be caught."

"She's right," Caelen adds. "The wolves will hear your boorish steps and catch wind of your scent from a mile away." He wrinkles his nose in disgust. "They will surely discover us if you accompany me."

I glower at Caelen. "I meant *both* of you."

He blinks at me. "Elves can travel unseen if we wish."

"Like you did when you followed me here?"

"Forgive me." He sighs heavily. "I saw you on your balcony that night. When you climbed down the tree, I was curious to know where you'd go."

I'm upset, but we do not have time to discuss it. "Since you are so good at hiding, take me with you back to the castle to search for Rina. I know the entire layout by heart."

I push myself up to sitting, but quickly fall back, hissing as sharp pain stabs at my side.

"You are in no condition to go." Caelen's green eyes sweep over my body in concern. "Your wound is still healing, Lyana. I will return to the castle and search for the queen, while you remain here and rest."

"I'm going with you, Elf, and that's that," Bran grumbles.

Caelen nods reluctantly before he leans over me and takes my hand. "I will return as soon as I can."

The tenderness in his expression is so foreign compared to the stoic mask he usually wears. Perhaps he feels guilty that I took the arrow instead of him. "All right. Be careful."

He motions to Bran, and they both leave the room.

I pray to the gods that Rina still lives.

CHAPTER 16

CAELEN

As the Dwarf and I make our way through the woods, I cannot stop thinking about Lyana. She risked her life to take the arrow that might have claimed mine. Why would she do this?

We barely know one another. We did not consummate our bond. She could have easily let me die. Instead, she saved me.

"You're fortunate she still lives, Elf," Bran's voice interrupts my thoughts. "If she dies, I'll have your head with my axe."

"Lyana will be fine," I state firmly. "I gave her my blood. She should be completely healed by morning."

He stops in his tracks, staring at me in disbelief for a moment before his expression shifts back into anger. "Well, I still don't trust you. If you ever so much as make her cry even one tear, I'll lop off your head faster than you can blink."

I look to the heavens and shake my head. "Are you going

to keep threatening me or are you going to help me find the queen?"

He lowers his brows. "Both."

I purse my lips and draw in a deep breath through my nostrils before exhaling in frustration. Dwarves are indeed stubborn, boorish, and unmovable—just as I have always been told.

"You know," Bran says, "I always heard that your kind has a touch of evil. When I saw those fangs and claws, I knew it was truth. Elves, Fae—the lot of you are villains."

"Many races have fangs and claws," I counter.

"You're right. Dragons, Fae, Elves, Wolves, Goblins, Trolls, Orcs..." He continues down a list of supernatural species. "You know what else you all have in common?"

I sigh but say nothing because he needs no additional encouragement.

"You're all villains with hearts of darkness."

I roll my eyes. It will do no good to argue with this simple-minded Dwarf.

"Nothing to say, huh?" he presses. "Is it because I've spoken the truth? Struck a nerve?"

My shoulders tense, but I stay silent.

"Tell me this, Elf," he growls. "Were you at least gentle with her?"

I turn to him. "What are you—"

I stop short. His eyes glitter with furious tears as he grits his teeth. It is as I suspected. This Dwarf is in love with Lyana.

In this moment, I actually *do* pity him.

"Not that it is your business, Dwarf, but nothing happened between us last night."

All the anger drains from his features as he blinks at me. "Truly?"

I nod.

He says nothing further, and I turn away as soon as I recognize the hope that burns in his eyes. I clench my jaw. Lyana is mine. She chose *me* as her husband, and I will not so easily surrender to a Dwarf.

When we reach the castle wall, I crouch low in the shadows. Bran stomps like a *turlayan* ox over to my side. I glower and hiss, "Could you at least *try* to be quiet?"

He narrows his eyes. "I *am* being quiet."

I heave another sigh as I return my gaze to the castle. If that is his notion of stealth, we will surely be caught.

A guard wearing Prince Fredrik's colors strides back and forth along the wall, disappearing around the corner for a minute before returning.

I point toward him. "That is our entrance."

Bran nods.

As soon as the guard disappears again, we scale the wall with the help of the thick vines. I move deftly but notice Bran struggling. I grit my teeth as he loses his footing and slams into the stone.

He quickly rights himself, and we continue climbing until we have hauled our weight over the top. We clamber down the inner wall and drop to the ground. Ice freezes my veins when I notice the king's dead body, hanging from a tree. Several burning torches surround him so that all may easily look upon the man who was their sovereign and know that he is dead.

"We cannot leave him hanging there," Bran whispers, pain twisting his expression. "King Gareth was an honorable man."

He is right. They have desecrated the king's body. The old gods will be unable to find his soul if he is left to hang in dishonor. He will be doomed to wander the earth as a lost spirit forever.

"He needs the proper rites for the gods to accept him. We

should at least burn his body; not leave him to rot like this," Bran insists. My brows rise at his words, and he frowns. "Did you think our people had forgotten the old ways?"

I say nothing as he continues. "The humans may no longer keep to them, but we do." He shakes his head, then returns his attention to the gruesome display before us. "At least, thank the gods, the queen is not hanging beside him. That means she could still be alive."

"Let's go," I whisper as one of the men guarding the tree moves away, leaving an open path to the castle.

As we enter, I'm surprised at how easily we slip through. Considering how many guards pursued us last night, I expected more roaming the hallways. Bodies of Eryadon soldiers litter the floors as we pass. I notice the broken and bloodied forms of my people as well. The scent of iron and death is so thick in the air, I can taste it upon my tongue. So many died last night.

I search for the area where I left Ruvaen, but see nothing. I do not know where he fell or what they may have done to his body. My hands curl into fists at my side. Fredrik will pay for this. I swear it to the old gods.

Sadness fills me anew when we come upon another of my kin, his gaze fixed and unseeing. I kneel beside him and close his eyes as I whisper. "May the gods carry you to the ever-lasting kingdom beyond all pain and sorrow."

I stand, and Bran grimaces with pity before we continue on our way.

When we reach the royal chambers, the door is ajar. Carefully, I push through, and we slip inside to find the queen lying upon the bed, her eyes closed in sleep.

There is a long chain attached to her ankle. No guards watch her, however, so I rush forward to set her free. My skin burns the moment my hands touch the metal. *Iron.* It is poison to my kin. Bran, however, is unaffected.

He huffs. "The rumors are true, then?" he asks.

I narrow my eyes. "Hurry."

"My queen," he hisses. "We're here to free you."

Her eyes fly open, and panic steals over her features before her gaze settles on his face. "Bran. Where's Lyana?"

"Safe. In the mountain," he answers. "That's where we're taking you."

She sits up in bed. The harsh *crack* of the shackles breaking makes me wince. I worry the sound may carry down the hallway and alert one of the soldiers.

Once she is free, Bran gathers her in his arms and lifts her to his chest. "I can walk, Bran," she insists.

He shakes his head. "No, my queen. You are with child, and we must move quickly."

Together, we dart back down the hall as stealthily as we can. When we reach the exit, the queen turns and buries her face in Bran's chest to avoid the sight of the king's corpse.

A horse neighs, and I turn to find several beasts tied to their posts, fully saddled. The gates are wide open, and there are no guards in sight.

I cannot believe our good fortune. I suppose last night's swift victory has made Fredrik confident and careless.

I turn to Bran. "We can escape on horseback."

He nods.

Extending my nails into claws, I dash to the tree and cut down the king. I remove my tunic and drape it over his face and upper body. Grasping one of the nearby torches, I set fire to the fabric. Quickly, I whisper the sacred rites of passing to ease his journey from this life to the next.

Although I did not really know him, he was the father of my mate, and king of Eryadon. As such, he deserves so much more than this, but there isn't any time. We must see to the safety of his wife and unborn child.

I rush back to Bran and the queen.

He helps her onto one of the horses, then he and I take two more. He nods to show me he is ready, and we dig our heels into the horses' sides, racing to the gates.

The galloping hooves of our escape draw attention. Alarm bells clang through the air as guards shout from all sides. "Stop them! They're getting away!"

We press our horses harder. I dare not look back for fear that they follow closely on our heels. As we disappear beneath the thick canopy of the forest, hoofbeats thunder at our backs, twigs breaking and leaves crunching.

I motion to Bran, gesturing for him to follow as I turn down a path that twists and winds through the trees to throw them off our trail.

The sound of running water catches my attention, and I lead us toward it. Wolf shifters have an exceptional sense of smell, but if we travel through the water, we have a chance of losing them.

When we reach the water, I am stunned at just how wide and fast the river roars before us. This will be more difficult than I anticipated.

My horse tosses his head in protest, so I place a gentle hand on his mane. "Be calm, my friend. We can make it. I know we can."

"Easy for you to say, Elf," he replies sarcastically in my head. *"You see how swift that current is just as I do."*

I sigh. It seems my horse is the surly sort. I address him. "I was not implying you are simple-minded. I was merely trying to inspire confidence."

"Are you talking to the horse?" the queen asks.

I nod, but Bran interjects, "Elves are able to commune with many creatures. It's unnatural, if you ask me."

I cross my arms and sigh. "And I suppose the stone whispering you Dwarves do, when you mine and build things, is natural now, is it?

Bran narrows his eyes.

My horse snorts in an approximation of a laugh.

I swing my leg over his back and drop to the ground, grabbing his bridle. I choose to ignore Bran's comment as I address my horse aloud again. "I'll lead you across. I will not add to your burden."

He dips his massive head. *"Thank you. Now I feel as though we have a chance."*

As we wade into the water, the current pulls at us, trying to swallow us into the river's depths. Bran leads his horse and the queen's, while she stays mounted.

When we reach the other side, I turn to my horse. "Are you all right?"

He nods as his critical eyes travel over my form. *"It's cold in the forest,"* he comments, and I understand he does not wish me to ride him now that we're both completely drenched.

I sigh. "Worry not. I'll continue to walk."

Sure enough, as we draw closer to the mountain, I no longer hear the sound of horses or men in pursuit behind us. It seems our plan worked, and we have lost them.

Bran takes the lead. "I know a secret entrance we may use." He turns back to me with narrowed eyes. "Can I trust you not to reveal it to your kin?"

I huff out an exasperated breath. "Despite what you may believe, I am *not* your enemy."

"Hmph," is all he replies before continuing.

I follow him through the forest. The entire area is thick with long, wiry branches that catch on our clothing like skeletal hands trying to hinder our progress. Wherever he is leading us, it is a path that is likely seldom traveled, given the thick vegetation and uneven ground.

We reach a cave entrance completely concealed by a mass of hanging vines. I knew the Dwarves possessed the ability to conjure illusory magic, but this is indeed impressive. If not for Bran, even *I* would never have found these doors in the side of the mountain.

He opens them and, as we pass through, a subtle tingling sensation moves over my skin. An effect of the magic, I suppose.

It feels like an eternity before we come upon a heavy metal gate. Bran raps a strange cadence against the doorway, and the gate opens a moment later. Two guards greet him warmly before glowering in my direction. Their eyes widen when they notice the queen on the horse behind us.

Their expressions turn somber, and they bow in respect to her as they allow us to pass.

"Where is Lyana?" Bran asks one of them.

"The princess is with your father in the throne room."

Bran helps the queen dismount and then guides us down a long corridor.

Glowing gemstones embedded in the walls provide enough light that it is as if we are standing outside despite being deep inside the mountain. We enter a wide cavern lined with massive support columns, carved with such precision they are truly impressive to behold.

Several dwarves stop and observe as Bran leads us to a set of large golden doors directly across the way, to what I assume is the hall of the king. The doors groan on their hinges as they swing open.

Lyana's head whips toward us. Relief inflates my chest. I am so glad to see her looking better. It seems that my blood is working to heal her quickly, because I notice she does not appear to be in pain when she moves.

The queen rushes toward her. Lyana throws her arms around her stepmother, and they both burst into tears.

Eventually, Bran leads the queen away, telling her she should rest and gather her strength.

I observe, from the shadows, as Lyana makes her way down the hallway and through a another set of golden doors. The etchings in the metal suggesting this is a place of worship.

Although I do not understand it, some primal instinct within me insists that I follow her. Perhaps it is because I gave her my blood—one of the most intimate acts among my people, and usually only shared with one's mate.

Before I can question it further, she walks inside and I quietly follow her.

CHAPTER 17

LYANA

My footsteps echo loudly as I walk through the empty chapel. I pass row upon row of stone benches. The soft illumination of the gemstones embedded in the walls cast the entire space in an ethereal glow.

Tears stream down my face as I approach the altar and light one of the candles. My gaze sweeps over the others that burn beside it. Sadness tightens my chest. Each of these is in remembrance of someone.

I drop to my knees and bow my head as I murmur the words of an ancient prayer my mother once taught me.

Absently, I touch my side, where my injury was. Dwarvish healing is impressive. Already my wound is closed and only a hint of pain still lingers in its place.

A soft cadence of steps behind me draws my attention. I turn and am surprised to find Caelen.

"You pray to the old gods," he says, and I recognize the

question in his statement. "I did not think humans still followed their ways."

"My mother did. She taught Arthur and me the prayers."

Caelen kneels beside me, his gaze fixed upon the altar.

"Bran told me what you did for my father." I struggle to keep my voice even despite my sadness. "Thank you for not leaving him like that... and for rescuing Rina."

His face is a perfect stoic mask, but his green eyes shine with pity as he dips his chin in a subtle nod.

He darts a glance at my side, where the arrow hit me. "You are feeling better?"

"Yes. My wound is already healed and the pain is almost completely gone."

"I am relieved," he says. "You have recovered much sooner than I had anticipated."

The doors open behind us and I turn to find Bran approaching. I stand. "How is Rina?"

"Resting." His gaze flicks to Caelen. "I've come to show you to your rooms."

My head throbs, from the stress of the past few days, as we follow him through the mountain. Several Dwarves eye Caelen with a strange mixture of wariness and outright anger visible in their features.

They probably believe I was forced into this marriage. The Dwarves are so loyal to me, I realize this kind of belief could put my new husband in danger. So, I slow my steps and wait for him to catch up. Without hesitation, I loop my arm through his as if it were the most natural thing in the world between us.

Caelen stops a moment, probably surprised by this sudden contact, before we continue on, following behind Bran.

As soon as I leave the main thoroughfare and turn down an empty hallway, I release my grip on Caelen's arm.

Bran stops before a door and turns to me. "Here's your room. Mine is next door if you need anything."

I'm touched by his thoughtfulness. "Thank you, Bran." I give him a warm hug. "I think I'll lie down for a bit."

He nods.

Caelen's steps echo behind me, and I turn just as Bran places a meaty arm in his path. "Leave her. Your room is farther down the hallway."

"She is my *mate*." Caelen grits his teeth.

"Let him go, Bran."

Bran's head jerks back in surprise, but he allows him to pass. Caelen follows me into the room and then closes the door behind us.

Without a word, I collapse on the bed. I curl onto my side and hug the pillow tightly to my chest. The mattress dips to one side as Caelen sits beside me. He rests a gentle hand on my shoulder.

"You don't have to do that, you know," I whisper, and he stills. "We never consummated our marriage. You are not bound to me if you do not wish to be."

"Why do you say this?" he asks.

I roll to face him. "You married me to ensure peace between our kingdoms. Fredrik has taken control. You do not need me anymore. My father is dead, my castle is gone, and—"

"It matters not," he interrupts. "You are my mate. We exchanged vows."

I sigh. "Those were words, Caelen. Nothing more."

His brow furrows deeply. "They were *sacred* vows," he corrects. "Did they mean nothing to you?"

I sit up. "I'm sorry, Caelen, but I hardly know you. I—"

"And yet you took my arm in front of the Dwarves... told your friend to let me pass so I might stay in the same room with you tonight." He pauses. "I know you did this to protect

87

me, Lyana. You're worried if I were alone, I'd wake up to a Dwarf standing over my bed with an axe in their hands."

A soft laugh escapes me. "Oh, Caelen, I do not think they would go that far."

He arches a brow, appearing unconvinced.

I laugh even harder, and a hint of a smile curls his lips before his expression sobers again.

"You took an arrow meant for my back. I owe you a life debt, at the very least. I will not abandon you, Lyana."

CHAPTER 18

CAELEN

Her gaze meets mine, full of disbelief. "I release you from your debt, then. You can return to your kingdom and forget about me."

"No, I cannot," I state firmly.

"Why?"

"We exchanged vows, Lyana," I explain. "I am a High Elf. The words were binding; we are now bound to each other."

Her jaw drops but she quickly snaps it shut. "Are you—are you saying that you cannot be released from the vows we made?"

"A deal made with my kind is not easily broken."

"But there is a way to do this?" she asks. "A way to free us both from our vows?"

Pain stabs at my chest as hope sparks in her gaze. I do not understand this despairing feeling. Is this not what I originally wanted? A way out from a marriage made solely for political reasons?

Reluctantly, I nod. "We would have to go to the Elders. It is… not something done lightly."

She frowns. "So… until we can go to one of the Elders, we're bound to each other?"

"Yes," I reply solemnly. "You are my mate and I am yours. We married to unite our two kingdoms; to avoid more needless bloodshed between our people. Eryadon is rightfully yours, and I will help you take it back."

Her golden-brown eyes search mine. "Why would you do this for me?"

"You are not the only one who lost someone, Lyana. All of my party, including my mentor, Ruvaen—the man who practically raised me and my siblings—were slaughtered by Fredrik's guards. I will not allow their deaths to go unpunished."

She studies me with a piercing gaze as I continue. "You said marriages among your kind could be annulled if there is no proof of consummation."

She nods.

"When we arrive at my kingdom, we will forgo the Elven ceremony of bonding and instead lead our armies back to your lands. After that, we can annul the marriage and form an alliance between our two kingdoms."

She studies me a moment, her brows drawn together in deep contemplation.

"I would know your answer," I press.

"Yes," she replies. "My answer is yes. I give you my word that I will honor and hold to an alliance with Rivenyl."

I dip my chin in a firm nod. "Then, we are agreed."

She extends her hand and I take it in mine. I recognize the human gesture to agree upon a deal. Although, as my gaze drops to her soft, pink lips, I wish we were sealing our bargain in the old ways of my people, as we did at our wedding: with a kiss. "Thank you, Caelen."

After she agrees to my plan, she lies back down and turns onto her side.

I gather a few pillows, intending to sleep upon the floor, but she stops me. "You can stay here," she says, a nervous smile on her face. "I trust you not to try anything."

A grin tugs at my lips as she places two pillows between us anyway. As if that could stop me if I were the monster she, no doubt, first believed that I was. I am glad, however, that she trusts me enough to know I will not harm her.

I lie on my back, staring up at the ceiling. I listen as they rhythm of her breathing becomes soft and even.

After a while, I close my eyes, intending to drift away. My nostrils flare as I detect the saline scent of her tears, and I open them again and glance at her.

My heart clenches. She is crying in her sleep. My bride has been through much. She has lost her mother, her brother and now her father as well. I am glad, at least, that we were able to return Rina to her.

Carefully, I pull the comforter up over her, tucking it around her shoulders. She nestles beneath the blanket and I remain awake a bit longer to make sure she does not need anything. I understand all too well the cost of grief. If there were a way to spare her this, I would. But, because there is not, I will do whatever I can to help her.

We are bound to each other. And until she dissolves our bond, I will not forsake my mate.

CHAPTER 19

LYANA

When I wake in the morning, Caelen is still asleep. Quietly, I leave the bed and go into the cleansing room to dress. I'm glad when I find a dress tunic and a pair of leggings and boots already waiting for me.

Because they are meant for a Dwarf woman, they're a bit large on me, but I do not mind. They're comfortable and easier to move in than a regular dress.

I notice my blade on a nearby table. The memory of when Caelen first presented it to me flashes through my mind as I tuck it into my belt.

As soon as I'm ready, I tiptoe from the room and out into the hallway. I make my way to Bran's door and knock lightly.

The door flies inward almost immediately and I'm shocked to see Bran standing before me, his eyes bloodshot and with heavy, dark circles under his lids. "Are you all right? Did he hurt you?"

I roll my eyes. "I'm fine, Bran. Caelen did not hurt me."

A rumbling growl rises in his throat as he steps out into the hallway, eyeing the door to my room. "Where is he?"

"Asleep." I purse my lips. "Are you going to grumble all day, or are you going to come with me?"

His head jerks back. "Where are you going?"

I start down the hallway and call over my shoulder. "To check on Rina." I swallow back a sob. "She is with child and she recently lost her husband."

Bran's large hand on my shoulder stops me abruptly, and I turn to face him. His eyes shine with sadness. He pulls me into a hug. "I'm sorry, Lyana. Truly. Your father was a good man."

Tears gather in the corners of my eyes, but I blink them back. "Thank you, Bran."

When we reach Rina's room, I knock gently on the door, but no one answers. Carefully, I push it open and am surprised to find her bed doesn't appear to have been slept in. "That's strange," I murmur, more to myself than to Bran. "Where could she be?"

"Perhaps she couldn't sleep." He shrugs. "She has to be here somewhere though. We'll find her."

I nod and we continue on toward the main caverns. Silently, we walk side by side toward the gardens. I've always been enchanted by this place. As we step inside, I study the glowing vegetation in wonder.

Mushrooms as tall as a man line the walkways, glowing with a soft blue bioluminescence. A small stream of water flows along the pathway, winding through the gardens. Dwarf children skip along the gravel walks, laughing and chasing each other under the watchful eyes of their parents.

When we reach the large fountain near the center, a memory of my father standing before it returns. He was as enchanted with this place as I was.

The painful image of his body, dead and bleeding on the floor resurfaces, springing tears to my eyes. Clenching my jaw, I push them down and curl my hands into fists at my side as I think on Prince Fredrik. "I'm going to kill him, Bran."

"Caelen?" he asks. "Good. I'll help."

Surprised by his answer, I whip my head toward him, and a smile tugs at my mouth. He's always done this, ever since we were children. Always trying to lighten my sadness with his joking. "Not *Caelen*. Fredrik," I correct.

"I agree. We'll kill him too. Right after Caelen," he adds with a teasing smirk.

I roll my eyes. "Will you please be serious for a moment?"

"I am," he says innocently, an amused glint in his eye. "Why do you believe otherwise?"

"Oh, Bran, stop it," I gently chastise. "Caelen's not the villain you think he is."

"Aye. I'll have to admit there may be some truth to that."

"Oh?" I ask, his answer surprising me. "Why the change of heart?"

His gaze slides to mine, all traces of his teasing now gone. "He gave you his blood to heal you."

A hazy memory floats to the surface of my mind of Caelen biting into his wrist and forcing his blood to my mouth when I was injured. "I... remember that now."

"It is never done for Outsiders. *Ever*," he adds for emphasis. "Not that I've heard of anyway. Or, at least, not for a number of years."

A frisson of fear travels down my spine. "Why not?"

"It's like giving you a piece of himself, Lyana."

I frown. "What do you mean?"

"I saw what he was doing when I came upon you. When I told the Healer, she was shocked. She said the High Elves used to do this for their human brides. It would extend their lives to match that of their own, and grant them similar healing abilities like the Elves as well."

I stare at him in astonishment. "You mean... I'll live as long as a High Elf now?"

"As long as any Otherworldly creature, in fact," he replies. "Dwarves included."

I'm completely stunned by this information. Caelen said nothing of this. "Why would he do this?"

Bran shakes his head. "*That*, I do not know."

High Elves and Otherworldly beings have long lives. Much longer than that of any human. Caelen did not have to do this. He could have easily let me die from my injury.

"It's the only thing that stayed my axe when I came upon you that night," Bran says, pulling me back from my thoughts. "When I first saw you in his arms, lying so still, I thought—" His voice catches. "I thought the worst."

"So... you trust him then?" I ask, uncertain.

"Hmmph," he grumbles. "He's a High Elf. They do nothing save that which will benefit them." He turns to me and changes the subject. "Come on. Let's go practice," he says with a lopsided grin. "We'll see if your aim has improved any since our last lesson."

"I do not have time to practice, Bran. I need to start formulating a plan to retake the throne."

"My people will help," he says. "But we'll need reinforcements from the Dwarves of the Ferylan Mountains to aid us. Father has already sent word to them. It will take at least a few days to hear back. In the meantime,"—he motions for me to follow him—"we'll practice your skills with the bow and arrow."

As I follow him out of the gardens, my thoughts return to my new husband. At first, I was afraid of marrying a former enemy. But after the time I've spent with him, and what Bran just told me, I am beginning to believe most of what I heard about his people may have been entirely wrong.

CHAPTER 20

CAELEN

W hen I awaken, Lyana is no longer in bed next to me. I sit up and draw in a deep breath. Her scent still lingers here, telling me she left not long ago.

I go to dress and wrinkle my nose in disgust at the Dwarvish attire that has been laid out for me. Not only is the coarse fiber rough against my skin, but it smells so much of Dwarf, I cannot imagine having to wear this for longer than a few hours.

The simple earthen gray and brown tones of the tunic, pants and boots are so dull it is no wonder Dwarves are always in a foul mood. Dressing themselves in such plain and muted colors must take an effect upon one's soul.

I step out into the hallway and follow Lyana's scent through the labyrinth of corridors. I reach a set of golden doors with the etched symbols of an axe, a bow and arrow, and a sword. I push them open and am surprised to find a training area of some sort with weapons lined up along the far wall.

I notice several Dwarves paired off and sparring with each other, but it is the figure in the distance that draws my attention. It is Lyana, standing tall and proud with a bow. With an arrow nocked in the bowstring, I watch as she takes careful aim and then lets it fly.

The arrow hits slightly off center from the target, and I watch in awe as she releases another, this time hitting closer to her intended mark.

I am impressed. I did not know my mate was a warrior, but I probably should have. Dhurvaen said her brother, Arthur, was one of the most skilled warriors he had ever seen.

As I make my way across the training grounds to reach her, I find myself wondering what else I do not know about my mate.

When she turns and her luminous golden-brown eyes meet mine, I realize that—despite my better judgement—I am most curious to find out.

"What do you want, Elf?" Bran steps between us.

"*Bran,*" Lyana levels a warning glare at him.

He sighs. "I meant to say *good morning,* Caelen."

I arch a brow, because I'm certain he did not mean to say this, but I let it go, and instead reply, "Good morning."

My eyes sweep to Lyana. "I came to speak with you about—"

"Bran," a voice calls out, interrupting me.

I turn to find another Dwarf walking toward us. "Your father wishes to speak with you and the princess."

Together, we follow him to what I assume are the king's private chambers.

King Edwyrd is seated at a large round table and Lyana's stepmother sits beside him. The entire room appears to have been dipped in gold, for it covers almost every surface and piece of furniture.

The king frowns as soon as his gaze lands upon me. He probably did not expect me to come. The message from his servant did not include my name in his summons, but I am glad this opportunity affords me to lay out my plans.

We each take a seat at the table. A large map is spread out before us, along with several carved wooden pieces that I can only assume represent armies.

I arch a brow when I notice two of them are red—the color of Edwyrd's banner. Another is blue, representing the army of Eryadon and the last is yellow for Fredrik's men.

There is no other on the board. I lift my gaze to the king and arch a brow. "You have no piece to represent Rivenyl."

He narrows his eyes. "Aye. I didn't think your people would bother with any of this."

His words are an insult. "Princess Lyana is my mate. My people will offer her aid."

Crossing his arms, he sits back in his chair. "Of course, you will. If we're successful in taking back the kingdom, I suppose you'd be wanting to make yourself king, then, now, wouldn't you?"

I clench my jaw. "Lyana is the rightful heir. I do not seek to take the throne from her."

What I don't mention is our conversation last night and how we discussed dissolving our bond. That is a private matter between us, and not something I feel particularly inclined to share. Especially with someone so hostile to me and my kin.

My gaze darts to her, wondering if she will volunteer this information. Her eyes meet mine and silent understanding passes between us before she turns her attention back to the king. "Caelen knew before our marriage that it would be my decision for him to either be king or consort."

I meet the king's gaze evenly. "I will return to my kingdom and gather my forces. I will—"

"You will not make it," Rina interrupts.

"Why not?"

"Fredrik has informed everyone that it was your guards who attacked in the night, and he and his men came to the rescue. They claim you murdered the king and stole the princess. The palace has issued a statement demanding your capture and death. You are a wanted man. You will not get far if you leave here."

I still. My heart squeezes painfully in my chest as I think of my father and younger sister. They will be devastated once they hear this. I know they would never believe that I killed the king and kidnapped Lyana, but they will be worried to no end for my safety.

I turn to the king. "I need to send word to my father and sister."

"Fredrik's men are posted all along the roads," King Edwyrd replies. "We were fortunate to be able to get at least one rider past them to the Dwarves of the Ferylan Mountains to ask for their aid." He looks to Lyana and Rina. "My cousin Dalwyn will send his forces to help retake the castle. I am certain of it."

"But how can you be sure the rider still lives?" Rina asks. "Just because he made it through one check point does not mean he was successful in reaching his destination."

She is right, and I can tell by the expression on Edwyrd's face that he has considered this as well. I lean forward. "All the more reason I must go to Rivenyl."

Rina shakes her head. "Fredrik has men searching for you and the princess." Her gaze darts to Lyana. "He will not stop until he finds and kills you both."

"Let him try," I grind out.

CHAPTER 21

LYANA

Caelen is determined to get back to his people despite Rina's warning. I understand his wanting to return to his home and his family, but I must find a way to convince him to stay. At least until I can spread truth of what really happened at the castle.

If he were to leave now, he would surely be caught and punished for crimes he did not commit.

Bran walks beside me as we cross the main hall. My mind keeps replaying the conversation with Bran's father—King Edwyrd. I wonder how long I will have to remain here while we wait for word from the Dwarves of the Ferylan Mountains.

When we enter another large cavern, I allow my gaze to travel over the glittering gemstones embedded in the walls. They provide almost as much light as the sun would during the day. I am thankful these beautiful rocks can provide such bright illumination for these great halls and caves. It is the only way I have ever been able to tolerate being inside the mountain despite my claustrophobia.

Dwarf children run past us, one bumping against my skirt. She lifts her little face to me. "Forgive me, Princess."

"It is all right." I smile. "I know it was an accident."

She beams and runs to join her friends.

My gaze tracks them to the far wall, where they skid to a halt as Caelen enters. All watch him warily, as if they expect him to attack or turn into a monster at a moment's notice.

Surely, he must notice their gawking, but he appears unaffected. With his chin tipped up and his hands clasped neatly at his back, he stares down imperiously as he passes.

One child backs away, tripping over a stone. Lightning fast, he catches her before she falls. She trembles as he helps her regain her balance. "Please, don't hurt me," she whimpers.

He lowers himself to one knee before her, leaning down even further until his face is level with hers. "Do not fear, Little One. My kind do not hurt children."

Her eyes widen. "Truly?"

He dips his chin. "Truly."

She studies him a moment. "Your ears are a lot more pointy than mine are."

A smile tugs at his lips. "The better to hear you with."

"My papa says Elves can speak to animals. Is that true?"

He nods, arching a brow. "And I've heard Dwarves can whisper to stones."

She tips up her little chin. "I'm going to be a stone whisperer just like my papa someday."

"And I am certain you will make a fine one," he says.

She lifts a tiny mouse from her pocket, its nose sniffing the air. "This is Teeny. Do you want to say hello?"

It's easy to see the smile he tries to suppress as he turns

his attention to the mouse, clearing his throat and forcing his expression into a serious one. "Hello, Teeny, it is lovely to meet you."

The mouse stands up on its hind legs and Caelen tips his head to the side as if listening.

"What did she say?" the little girl asks.

He grins. "She says your name is Sanna and she likes being your friend."

Her mouth falls open and then a beaming smile lights her face as she looks at her mouse. "I like being your friend too, Teeny."

My heart melts as she wraps her arms around Caelen. "Thank you, Mr. Elf."

I observe as he carefully returns her embrace. "You are most welcome, Sanna."

She turns and skips off to rejoin her friends.

"I didn't know he liked children," I murmur, more to myself than to Bran.

Bran crosses his arms over his chest. "Yes. Probably the same way witches with gingerbread houses like them too," he grumbles.

I roll my eyes in frustration.

Caelen joins us, silently acknowledging Bran before addressing me. "We should leave tomorrow at first light."

"Leave?"

"Yes. We must go to Rivenyl and gather the army. I will help you regain your throne and claim your vengeance."

"But, what about what King Edwyrd and Rina said about Fredrik's men?"

Bran steps between us, narrowing his eyes. "She'll not be going anywhere with you. Lyana is staying here where it's safe."

"It is not safe here for Lyana *or* the queen," Caelen states firmly. "We have to go. Fredrik's guards are probably on their way here even now."

"What makes you think that?" Bran asks.

Caelen clenches his jaw. "Because it would not take a sorcerer to figure out where we were headed when we escaped the castle. It is well known that the Kingdom of Eryadon is allied with your people."

"Rina's in no condition to travel," I point out. "She's only a few weeks away from her due date."

Caelen frowns. "You cannot remain here, and neither can the queen. If Fredrik's goal is to take over the kingdom, he cannot leave any of Eryadon's royal family alive. Don't you understand? It's not safe for you here."

His words ring with truth no matter how much I wish it were not so.

Bran plants his feet wide, thrusting out his chest. "They're much safer here than out there where they would no doubt be hunted by Fredrik and his men." He levels an icy glare at Caelen. "So if you want to go, that's fine. But Lyana and the queen are staying right here."

I move from behind Bran. "I appreciate you trying to keep us safe, Bran, but Caelen is right."

Bran gives me a wounded look that sends a sharp twinge of pain straight to my gut. "But, Lyana, you—"

I take his hand and squeeze it gently. "If we stay here, Fredrik will come looking for us, Bran. You know how much I care about you and your people. I cannot be responsible for placing any of you in danger. I could not live with myself if anything happened to you or your family because of me."

"Do you not know that each and every one of us would lay down our lives for you, Lyana?" His eyes shine with tears. "You saved us, and that has earned you a place here, and the protection of our kin."

I open my mouth to reply, but alarms ring out.

Bran's eyes widen. "Those are the sentry bells. We must be under attack."

A voice echoes through the corridors. "Prince Fredrik's men are here! They're trying to breach the entrance!"

CHAPTER 22

LYANA

"This way!" Bran calls over his shoulder. We follow closely behind him, rushing up the stone steps to the upper level and a balcony overlooking the outside gates.

Caelen, Bran, and I peer over the railing, and my jaw drops when I see Prince Fredrik and his army below, just beyond the mountain entrance.

I gasp, worried they'll see us, but then notice a subtle glow surrounding the balcony. It is a concealment spell, for I've never noticed this area when approaching the mountain. I knew the Dwarves were capable of illusory magic, but I have never seen it in use before now. Bran always said it was a closely guarded secret among his kind.

I watch as several of Fredrik's men carry a felled tree toward what should be a hidden entrance. Terror fills me when I realize they plan to use it as a battering ram.

My head whips to Bran. "How do they know where the entrance is? It's hidden. No one can find it but your people."

He shakes his head in disbelief. "There is no way they could have possibly known. It makes no sense."

We observe as they rush toward the entrance. A thunderous boom echoes up the mountain wall as they ram the doors.

Caelen wraps his hand around my forearm, pulling me behind him as if instinctively trying to protect me. He looks to Bran. "Will they hold?"

"I—" he starts but stops abruptly. His jaw drops as he stares down below.

I follow the line of his gaze and then gasp when I spot my stepmother on a horse beside Fredrik. "They have Rina! We have to save her!"

I freeze when she leans over and kisses Fredrik passionately. His palm splays possessively over her abdomen and the truth suddenly hits me.

My voice is barely a whisper as furious tears of betrayal sting my eyes. "Rina did this. She caused all this. Why?" Without thinking, I yell her name. "Rina!"

Her head snaps up. "Come out, Lyana! Surrender yourself and we will show you mercy!"

Caelen growls low in his throat.

"Why, Rina?" I call back. "Why would you do this?"

Instead of outright answering me, she clasps Fredrik's hand. "I do not expect you to understand."

Tears threaten to fall, but I blink them back. I curl my hands into fists at my sides. "You claimed you loved my father. You said you loved me like a daughter," I fling the words out accusingly. "Why would you do this?"

"I give you my word that we will not harm you, Lyana. You will live in comfort, but I cannot allow you to go free." She places a hand on her belly. "You are the last of Eryadon's royal line, and would threaten our right to rule. I cannot allow that."

The image of Fredrik's palm on her abdomen flashes through my mind, and I breathe out a shaking breath.

The child she carries is not my father's.

"And why should I trust you?" I spit out. "Your word means nothing!"

"You're surrounded," Fredrik shouts. "Give up or we will kill every last one of you."

"Never!" King Edwyrd retorts. "This is our mountain. This is our home. Wolf filth will not take it from us. Not this day nor any other."

Fredrik releases a war cry, and his men resume their assault upon the doors. We retreat into the mountain, where the hallways erupt into chaos, as Dwarves rush back and forth readying for battle.

Bran takes my hand. "Come. I will hide you."

Caelen stops him. "No. She is not safe here."

Bran glares venomously. "*We* will protect her."

"How long until he breaches those doors?" Caelen asks. "You know they won't stop until they have her. Your people will die, and she will be captured and killed. Is that what you want?"

He clenches his jaw. "No."

"Then you must listen to me. They want Lyana. I must take her with me."

He frowns. "No! The Dwarves of the Ferylan Mountains will come. They will unite with us in battle and we will fight them off."

Caelen meets his gaze. "And how long will it take for your brethren to arrive?"

"We can hold them off," Bran counters. "We can—"

"Lyana and I will travel to my kingdom. We will return with the Rivenyl army and—"

"And seize control of her throne anyway?" he asks. "No. She does not need your help. We will fight for her and—"

"And die before your help arrives, Dwarf!" Caelen snaps. "You saw the number of men Fredrik has out there. It is only a matter of time before they breach your mountain. And it will happen well before the rest of your kin arrive."

It's easy to read the indecision in Bran's eyes. Caelen holds his gaze. "You know I am right. They will not stop, and your people will die, unless they believe she is gone." He scans the glowing bubble of magic that surrounds the balcony before his gaze snaps back to Bran. "Make use of your illusory magic. Make Fredrik believe Lyana has fled and they will leave you and your mountain alone. At the very least, it will give you enough time for the others to arrive and join forces with you."

I turn to Bran. "I don't want your people to die for me, Bran. Caelen's right."

Bran takes my hands. "I do not trust him or his people. Why do you?"

"He was kind to me on our wedding night. He could have forced himself upon me, but he did not. He respected my choice, and he has done nothing but help me since then. Why should I doubt him? Why should you?" I peek at Caelen. "Simply because he is an Elf?"

Bran grits his teeth. "A High Elf," he corrects. "The Woodland Elves are a better lot than his. So are the Fae, for that matter."

"Enough!" I snap. "I know you hate the Elves, but you must realize that he is right. I cannot remain here. Your people will die." I squeeze his hands gently. "I'm going with him, Bran. I have to."

Bran wraps his arms around me. His familiar bear hug tugging at my heart and bringing tears to my eyes. "I cannot leave my people, Lyana. Please, do not go. I'll find a way to keep you safe."

"As much as you want to protect me, do you not think I

wish the same for you and your family, Bran? You are my best friend. I couldn't live with myself if anything happened to you because of me."

He gives me a reluctant nod. His eyes shift to Caelen, anger and fury burning behind them. "Guard her with your life or I will hunt you to the ends of the earth."

Caelen places his open palm to his chest. "I will protect her until my last breath."

Bran narrows his eyes. "I'll hold you to your word, Elf. Now, follow me."

CHAPTER 23

LYANA

Bran guides us to a tunnel in the back of the mountain. It's dark here and I notice there are not as many brightly lit stones embedded in the walls as are present in the main corridors and rooms of the mountain. I'm able to see, but just barely.

The walls feel as if they are closing in, and I struggle to take a deep breath. Closing my eyes, I force myself to fight back the panic deep inside. I cannot allow my fears to overwhelm me. I have to be strong. I cannot fall apart right now.

Caelen's warm hand finds mine. "Are you all right?" he whispers.

Unable to speak, I nod.

Bran looks to Caelen. "This route is known only to my people."

"I understand," Caelen replies. "I will reveal your secret to no one."

Bran holds his gaze a moment before he turns his attention back to me and places his hands on my shoulders. "I am sorry, Lyana. I know how you feel about dark and enclosed spaces, but this tunnel is safe. I promise. It narrows for a ways, then widens again before the exit. It's roughly two days travel to get through it."

I peer down the darkened corridor, swallowing thickly. Although I've been inside the mountain many times throughout the years of our friendship, the areas I have frequented have always been brightly lit, large caverns and wide hallways.

He hands us each a heavy pack with supplies.

"Where does it come out?" Caelen asks.

"Near the border of Solwyck."

Solwyck. Dragon fire scorched their kingdom, leaving much of it in ruin. Everyone knows how Princess Halla was able to slay the dragon and save her people, but at great cost to herself. They say she may never walk again.

I used to be close to her and her brother, Gerold, when we were children. Our mothers were cousins. I wrote to them several times since we first learned of the attack, but have heard nothing in return. But I also understand they are no doubt busy trying to rebuild their once prosperous and shining city.

Bran embraces me tightly and whispers in my ear, "We will watch every day for your return. We'll be ready to march with you to retake the kingdom."

Tears swim in my eyes. "Be safe, Bran."

"I will." He levels an icy glare at Caelen. "Remember your promise, Elf."

Caelen dips his chin, and we turn and enter the caves.

The path grows even darker the farther we walk, and I realize that Bran has forgotten once again that human night vision is poor. I can barely see anything in the gloom. I trace my hands along the rock wall for guidance and startle when Caelen slips his hand into mine. "Allow me to guide you."

"You can see clearly?" I ask before remembering his words on our wedding night.

"Nearly as well as I can in the light." Amusement laces his tone. "I honestly do not know how you humans have managed to survive as a species. You have no claws or fangs, poor vision and hearing, and—"

"Enough." I narrow my eyes in the direction of his voice. "Or should I start listing your flaws?"

"I doubt you'd find any." He chuckles. "We Elves are perfect compared to you humans."

Offended, I open my mouth to reply, but stop abruptly as he says, "I am merely teasing you, Lyana." He squeezes my hand. "I thought it might help ease your fears."

A smile curls my lips as I decide to tease him in return. I tip my chin up. "Well, the joke's on you, Prince Caelen of Rivenyl. Did you know that you snore?"

His head whips toward me. "I *most certainly* do not," he replies indignantly.

"*Yes,* you do," I insist. It's not the truth, but he doesn't know that. Besides, I need to find something to tease him about.

He's silent for so long I worry that I may have gone too far and actually offended him. Finally, he says, "Well, *you* are short."

"I am *not* short," I huff.

"If you were a pixie that statement might be true."

My jaw drops, but I quickly snap it shut. I'm about to tell him off when a strange scurrying noise draws my attention up ahead. Fear skitters up my spine, and despite my earlier irritation, I press closer to Caelen. "What is that?"

"You really cannot see much of anything, can you?" he asks, surprise in his voice. "It's not that far up ahead," he murmurs.

"What is it?" I hiss, annoyed that he hasn't answered me yet.

Before he can answer, the sound of claws scraping against stone echoes through the tunnel and my dress flutters against my ankle as something moves past. Panic zips through me and I scream, scrambling up Caelen's body, clinging to him for dear life.

"It's all right, Lyana," he says quickly. "It was only a mountain rat. It's gone now."

Only a mountain rat.

My heart pounds as I lift my head from his chest and scan the darkness. "I hate rats. Are you sure?"

"Yes." Caelen's breath is warm in my ear, sending a shiver through my body, but this time not one of fear.

Suddenly, I'm acutely aware of just how close we are. My legs circle his waist and he has one hand on my backside, holding me up, while his other arm wraps around my torso, my entire body molded to his.

With my chest pressed to his own, I can feel each beat of his heart. I lift my head, and in the dim light our eyes lock. Our lips are so close, his warm breath fans across my skin. He smells of cinnamon and spice, but his breath is something akin to mint.

His gaze drops to my mouth and his hold tightens on me a moment before he carefully relaxes his grip. "I'm going to lower you back to the ground," he says, his voice rough.

"All right," I reply in a breathless whisper.

I unwrap my legs from around Caelen's waist, and he carefully lowers my feet to the ground. His hands linger a moment on my arms as he makes sure I'm steady before letting me go.

A hot flush burns my cheeks, but I smooth my hands over my tunic, raise my chin, and clear my throat. "Thank you," I struggle to keep my voice even as my heart still hammers in my chest.

"Of course," he replies, his voice rich and smooth as he takes my hand, interlacing our fingers. "Are you ready to continue?"

I manage to nod. "Yes."

As we continue on, the tunnel grows even darker. It's nearly pitch-black now. If not for Caelen, I'd definitely be lost.

I'm unsure if it's merely my imagination, but it seems as though shadows move at the edge of my very limited vision. My fears are confirmed at the sound of claws scraping against stone. "More mountain rats?" I ask.

"Among other creatures," Caelen replies casually.

"Other creatures?" I squeak as panic tightens my chest. "What are you talking about?"

CHAPTER 24

CAELEN

I realize my answer was the wrong one as Lyana stops in her tracks, her eyes wide. My nostrils flare as the acrid scent of her fear permeates the air. "What other creatures are there, Caelen? Please tell me there aren't any spiders."

I blink as I take in our surroundings. Thick webs line the cavern, and beastly, multi-faceted eyes study me in the darkness as several spiders, the size of mountain rats, observe us pass. Walking ahead of her, I've been pulling down the webbing as we advance, so she must not have felt it. I do not want her to be afraid, however. "No," I lie. "We are safe here."

A heavy sigh of relief escapes her. "Thank the gods. If you had said there were spiders in here, I think I would have had a panic attack and died."

Alarm sparks through me. "Humans can die from fear?"

"I certainly think so," she replies, and I swallow nervously.

I eye the spiders with an icy glower, silently warning them to stay away. Though Elves can communicate with animals, simple creatures like these only understand base emotion. So, I threaten them with wrath if they dare cross our paths or touch us. Sensing my warning, the spiders retreat into the rock crevasses.

The acrid scent of her fear is thick in the air. I decide to try to distract her with conversation.

A smile tugs at my lips as her golden-brown eyes meet mine. "I did not know my wife was afraid of rats."

She narrows her eyes. "It startled me."

A smirk twists my mouth. "Fortunate for you that you have a tall husband, then, is it not?"

Peeling laughter spills from her lips, and I am completely and utterly enthralled.

Soft light glows in the distance ahead, and I move toward it. When we get closer, I lift my gaze to find a hole in the ceiling. Pale moonlight spills in from above, forming a circle of light on the stone floor.

Mountain spiders hate light, so this is the ideal place to stop for the night. "We should rest here," I tell her.

As she steps into the circle, she looks up at me. The silvery beams cast her lovely features in an ethereal glow as I study her, completely transfixed.

She regards me a moment before lowering her eyes and nervously tucking a stray tendril of long black hair behind her ear. "We should unpack," she says.

I clear my throat and nod. I remove my pack and carefully unroll the bedding, laying it down on the floor. I pull out some bread and cheese and a waterskin.

My brows furrow as Lyana extracts her bedroll and places it across from me instead of next to mine. Does she not realize how cold it will be this evening? Even now, the temperature is already dropping.

"I thought we might sleep together this night," I say.

Her head snaps up and she opens her mouth, but only a

slight strangled sound escapes. A pink flush spreads across her cheeks and the bridge of her nose. "I—I thought we had agreed that our marriage would remain... unconsummated."

"Oh," the word leaves my lips in a rush as understanding fills me. "No—not like that," I quickly reassure her. "I was not referring to joining, I only meant for us to conserve warmth."

A huff of air escapes her in a nervous laugh. "Oh, thank goodness."

I'm not sure whether to be offended by her statement or not. I have always been considered rather handsome, even among my own kind. Does she not realize how many High Elf women would have gladly taken me as their mate?

I observe as she moves her bedding next to mine and sits cross-legged before me. We eat in silence as she scrutinizes the space around us. I wonder how much she can actually see beyond the soft light. I had no idea humans had such poorly developed night vision.

I am grateful, however, that she cannot see the several sets of eyes that study us from the shadows. I doubt she'd be able to sleep if she knew.

"I'm glad we found this patch of light," she murmurs. "I've always hated the dark."

I arch a brow. "Fortunate for you that you did not marry a Dwarf or a Dark Elf, then," I tease. "Or else you'd be making your home deep in the mountains."

She laughs—the sound light and airy like chimes and completely enchanting. "Yes, I suppose you're right." She grins. "And what sort of home does a High Elf live in?"

"Any High Elf, or me?" I ask, a smile tugging at my mouth.

"Both," she replies, her expression one of curiosity.

"Why? Do you plan on running away with one of my guards, or perhaps even a farmer, when we arrive?" I tease her again. "It would be quite a scandal if my mate ran off with another."

She laughs. "Is it not scandal enough that you wed a human?"

I arch a brow. "It is not as strange as you might think. Our kind used to intermarry all the time before the last Great War."

Her expression sobers. "You gave me your blood when I was injured. Bran said this is how High Elf Lords used to extend the lives of their human mates to match their own."

"This is true," I reply solemnly.

Her small brow furrows softly. "You've saved me twice now, Caelen."

I understand the question she does not ask, because it is one that I, myself, have wondered. At the time, I acted upon instinct. She was fading and I could not stand by and watch her die. Something about her calls to me. As if our souls are somehow connected, but I do not understand why.

Rather than tell her this, I offer a half-truth instead. "I swore an oath to you the day we met. I gave you a knife with my blood. Such a vow is not given lightly. It is sacred among my kind."

"You swore to protect me and to never harm me, Caelen. What you did goes far beyond that."

I meet her gaze evenly. "If you are asking if I regret sharing part of my life force with you, I do not. My vows to you were binding and I hold to them still."

CHAPTER 25

LYANA

His gaze holds mine intently. Caelen is not what I thought he was. He isn't the monster I grew up hearing about when people told stories of the High Elves. In truth, he is everything I could have wished for in a husband. He is kind, caring, intelligent, handsome.

If things had been different, I believe my father was right. Love could have followed from our union. But as I study Caelen, I remember that we made a deal. We both went into this marriage for the good of our kingdoms, and nothing more.

Besides, I'm sure he would prefer a High Elf wife, just as I am sure that life would probably be easier with a human husband. And yet, as I study him, I cannot help but wonder what it might be like to stay with him.

"We should rest," he says, breaking the silence between us.

He's right. We have a long day ahead of us tomorrow.

The air is much colder now that night has fallen and it

seems to be growing steadily worse. I lie down and pull the blanket over my shoulder, but it doesn't really help.

"We should sleep together to stay warm," Caelen says, removing his tunic.

I understand what he's saying, but as my gaze travels over his broad shoulders and the hard planes of muscle that line his abdomen and chest, I'm not entirely sure that's a good idea. When he removes his pants, leaving him only in his underwear, I swallow thickly and avert my eyes.

"You should undress as well," he says. "Skin-to-skin contact is best to keep warm."

A slightly strangled noise escapes me before I find my voice. "I—are you sure?"

He cocks his head to the side. "Have you never slept outside in the cold before?"

"You have?"

"Many times while traveling with our army."

Of course. I forget sometimes that his people have been fighting the Orcs and... my kind off and on for years. I'd heard Caelen and his brother had both seen their fair share of battle, but I hadn't really thought about it before now.

Hesitantly, I pull my tunic dress up over my head, holding it in front of my chest for a moment as I struggle to calm my racing heart. I wore far less than a bra and underwear on our wedding night, but this feels different because now I can see.

Drawing in a deep breath, I lower my tunic and carefully fold it, placing it to one side. I remove my leggings and fold them as well. I'm too embarrassed to look at Caelen because I know he's probably watching me, just as I was observing him earlier when he undressed.

He clears his throat and my eyes snap up to his. He offers me a faint smile and holds the blanket up for me to join him. "If you lie on your side with your back to me, that would probably be best."

I swallow hard and nod before curling onto my side. Carefully I scoot back, tensing for the moment I'll reach him.

My pulse pounds in my ears. Heat radiates from his body against my back and I know I'm close. I gasp as he wraps an arm around my waist and tugs me the rest of the way back against him. "Hey!"

"At the rate you were moving, you were more likely to freeze to death before you got over here."

"That is *not* true. I was almost there." I glance over my shoulder as I tease him. "But *someone* got impatient because he's cold."

He laughs softly in my ear. The movement of his body against mine causing a rather inconvenient tightening in my lower abdomen.

His athletic frame is warm and solid as he molds himself to me, nearly swallowing my form with his much larger one. He tucks his knees up behind mine and I place my feet between his calves. He inhales sharply. "Your skin is freezing."

A huff of laughter escapes me. "And you're like a furnace." I twist my neck to look back at him. "You were the one to suggest this. It's too late to change your mind," I tease, all the tension leaving my body. "I quite like it here."

"Of course, you would." He chuckles softly. "You're getting the much better part of this arrangement. While I'm stuck lying beside a block of ice."

I laugh again.

I am still shivering slightly and he tugs me even closer in response. "Do not worry. You should warm up soon."

Every inch of my body hums in awareness of his move-ments behind me as his entire form is flush against my own. From the rise and fall of his chest to the pounding of his heart against my back and the warmth of his breath in my ear as he speaks in his deep, smooth voice.

"Do you think any more mountain rats will bother us while we sleep?" I ask, trying to take my mind off his nearness.

"No. I have threatened them with a fiery death if they do not stay away."

I still and look back to him again. "Fiery death? Are you able to conjure flame? I thought the treaty bound your magic."

"It does." A smile tugs at his lips. "Signed in blood, the treaty with your kingdom binds my magic while in Eryadon, but what do mountain rats know of such things?"

Another laugh bubbles up. It seems my husband possesses more wit than I first realized. "What would happen if you did try to use your magic, anyway?"

He sighs. "I cannot conjure it at all. The treaty created a binding spell that renders me and my people unable to access our powers."

"Oh," I reply, wondering why the High Elves would ever agree to sign the treaty with this condition upon it.

"It was the only way your people would agree to peace," he adds, answering my unspoken question. "The document itself is kept in your castle's library. The binding spell was created so that it could not be broken unless your father or you tore the treaty in half."

Gently, I squeeze his forearm. "If I regain my throne, we can forge a new treaty, and I'll take away this condition on our agreement."

He stills. "You would do this?"

I nod, and then turn just enough to give him a faint smile. "If I cannot trust my own husband, who *can* I trust?"

A handsome smile lights his face.

Thoroughly exhausted, I close my eyes, allowing myself to slip into that space between wakefulness and dreams.

"Sleep now, Lyana," his breath is warm in my ear as his strong arm tightens around my waist, "I will keep you warm and safe."

With a deep sigh, I drift away into sleep.

CHAPTER 26

CAELEN

She is fragile, my human mate. More so than I realized. She probably would have died of cold this night, if she were traveling alone. The thought settles like a heavy weight in my chest as I regard her.

A smile tugs at my lips as I study the softly curved shell of her ear—so different from my own. If we were to have had children, I wonder whose features they would have inherited. Mine or hers?

I reflect on all that has happened. I hate that she is alone in the world. I cannot imagine being with no family. My thoughts turn to Bran. She considers him a best friend, but it is easy to see he regards her as much more.

I wonder how long after our annulment he'll wait before making his feelings known and approaching her about becoming her mate.

The thought burns like bitter acid in my throat as jealousy twists deep inside me. She does not want me, and I must accept this. She said as much when we discussed our marriage earlier. I entered into this arrangement believing that ours would be a union based solely upon political gain for both our sides.

However, when we married, I'd thought her human vows to love, honor and cherish me were as binding to her people as the words of the Elvish ceremony are to mine. So, I had already softened my heart toward her before discovering too late that I was mistaken.

And now, I find myself in an impossible situation. I actually care for her. I had not planned on this.

Even as I think this, I know it is not entirely correct. My feelings extend beyond simply caring. I am falling for her. This leaves me with only two choices. I must either force myself to let her go or convince her to be mine.

Closing my eyes, I send out another mental threat to the creatures that watch us from the shadows, warning them to stay away or suffer my wrath. When I'm satisfied they've retreated further into the rock, I let myself drift away.

When I wake in the morning, she is still fast asleep. The soft light of early dawn filters in from above, casting her in an almost ethereal glow.

She shivers slightly and I instinctively tighten my arm around her waist, pulling her close. She responds by nestling further into me.

Before I even realize what I'm doing, I gently nuzzle her hair and inhale deeply of her delicate scent.

Mine. The word flashes through my mind as a low rumbling growl vibrates my chest. Everything about her calls to me. The soft press of her body to mine, her scent, the memory of her smile.

With a heavy sigh, I push away these errant thoughts. She

does not want me. She desires to break our bond and be free of our marriage. I force myself to pull away and stand.

Carefully, I tuck the blankets up around her shoulders as I scan the cave. I issue another warning to the spiders that observe us from the darkness. In searching their intent, I find only curiosity, not danger or hunger, but I know Lyana would not understand this. So, I order them to stay back under threat of death.

Wanting to take my mind off Lyana, I quietly dress and decide to scout ahead a bit. I leave my boots behind so as not to waken her with the sounds of their steps.

I haven't gone very far when a piercing shriek echoes down the tunnel, stopping my heart in my chest.

Without hesitation, I race toward the ear-splitting sound to find Lyana whacking at a spider with one of my boots. I reach for the spider in my mind to make it retreat, but too late.

With a sickening crunch, she squashes it with my boot. I wrinkle my nose at the green goop now splashed across the leather. A large glop of spider entrails slides off my boot and slaps on the stone floor. *I loved those boots.*

Her triumph is short-lived, however, as several other spiders takes its place. She grabs my other boot.

"Lyana!"

"Caelen!" She spins and rushes forward, climbing up my body in a desperate attempt to escape.

Fierce protectiveness fills me as I hold tightly to her and glare at the spiders, sending a threat full of rage, promising a swift death if they do not retreat immediately. I will not have anything scaring her if I can help it.

I watch in satisfaction as they scurry back into the shadows. "They should leave us alone now," I inform her.

I hold her securely, oddly relishing the weight of her soft, pliant body plastered against me. Dressed only in her underwear and bra, my hand cups her backside to give her support as I hold her close. Her heart pounds against my chest.

"Are you sure?" she asks.

"Yes."

A smile tugs at my lips as her golden-brown eyes meet mine. "I promised them a swift death, like I did with the others. It kept them away until now. I think perhaps, because I had traveled further on, they—"

"*What* others?" She levels an accusing glare at me. "You *told me* there weren't any spiders in here."

I have made a mistake.

I move quickly to explain myself, hoping to avoid her wrath. "After your reaction to the rat, I did not think it wise to bring the spiders to your attention."

She narrows her eyes as she pushes away from me. I lower her feet to the ground and she stomps toward her folded clothing.

"And here I thought you were being the perfect husband," she murmurs under her breath.

She thought I was perfect? My chest swells with pride.

"But I guess I was wrong," she continues mumbling to herself in a voice so low I almost miss it. My chest quickly deflates at her words.

I know she is angry with me and that I should avert my eyes from her partially nude form, but I cannot force myself to look away. My mouth goes dry as I stare appreciatively at the sensuous curve of her breasts and the gentle flare of her hips.

She pulls the tunic over her head and then glares up at me. "Do you mind?"

My entire body flushes with heat as I stumble over my words. "Of—of course. Forgive me." I quickly lower my gaze to the floor.

I move to retrieve my boots, sighing heavily as I hold up the one covered in green goo.

"I'm sorry about your boot," she offers.

My gaze goes to her boots as I remember they were right next to mine. As if sensing my unspoken question, she shrugs. "Yours are bigger. Better for squashing monsters."

I raise my brows, and she laughs. "Don't look at me like that. They're just boots."

"I rather liked that pair of boots. They were the only thing I had that does not stink of Dwarf."

She rolls her eyes in mock irritation. "I'll wash them for you later, all right?"

My lips twitch as I tease. "I doubt any amount of soap and water will cleanse them now."

Laughter bubbles up from her throat, and it is the most enchanting sound I have ever heard. "I did not know Elves could be so dramatic."

I purse my lips even as a smile threatens to break free. "I believe you are confusing my kind with the Fae. You have not seen drama until you've spent some time amongst them."

She laughs some more. "Good thing I'm married to an Elf then, isn't it?"

My heart stutters as her lips curve into a stunning smile. "Yes, it is."

CHAPTER 27

LYANA

As we walk through the tunnel, the light grows dim again, making it difficult for me to see clearly. Caelen takes my hand. Threading his fingers through mine, he pulls me along behind him.

It takes a while before his boot stops squelching with each step. I listen as he bemoans that the fine leather is ruined beyond repair now. Although, I suspect he does this to tease me and keep my mind off the darkness and the sounds of skittering creatures moving in the shadows beyond my vision.

Caelen stops abruptly, and panic flutters in my chest. "What is it?"

"The ceiling dips. We will have to crawl. Wait a moment," he says as he releases my hand. "I will have to get some rope from my pack."

"Rope? For what?"

"So I will not lose you in the narrow tunnel."

I swallow hard as panic begins to build in my chest.

The sound of fabric rustling echoes along the walls as he searches his bag. Once he finds the rope, he ties it around my waist. "I will tie the other end to myself so you can follow me."

I glance behind him at the narrow opening that disappears into solid black. Dark memories flood my mind of the time I spent trapped in a well, when I was a child. I draw in a shaking breath. "Caelen, I don't think I can go in there."

He takes my hands in his. "Yes, you can."

When he tries to pull me toward it, I shrink back. "Caelen," I struggle to keep my voice even. "Wait."

Gently, he squeezes my hands, his callused thumbs moving in soothing circles across my knuckles. "You can do this, Lyana." His voice is warm and smooth like velvet. "I will be with you the entire time. I will not let anything happen to you."

"You promise?" My voice comes out barely a squeak.

Tears gather in my eyes, but I blink them back. I'm ashamed of my fear, and I hate appearing weak.

"I promise," he whispers softly.

Together, we get on our hands and knees, and I crawl through the darkness, completely blind and utterly terrified. The hard rock seems to close in around me more tightly with each breath as we squeeze through.

My pulse pounds in my ears, drowning out all other noise as I pull myself along the cold, stone floor. I focus on the taut rope around my waist, anchoring myself to the firm tug of it around my body, reminding me that I'm not alone.

Without warning, it goes slack. Panic seizes my heart. "Caelen!"

"Lyana, the rope came loose. I'm retying it."

My chest rises and falls rapidly as I struggle to breathe. It feels as though the walls are closing in on me. Blindly, I reach out with my hand and find only hard stone.

Unbidden tears escape my lashes as dark memories return. Caelen's warm hand finds mine. The hard calluses of his palm scraping softly across mine as he entwines our fingers. "Lyana, it's all right," he whispers.

I squeeze my eyes shut, trying to push down my tears. "Caelen." My voice quavers. "I just need a moment. I can do this. I can do this," I repeat the whispered words, trying to shore up my courage.

I hate my fear and I hate feeling weak. This isn't who I am.

Drawing in a deep breath, I slowly exhale, trying to calm my heartrate and breathing. I think of my mother, my brother, and my father. My family is gone. I'm all alone. I need to be stronger than this. I *have* to be.

"You are not alone," Caelen's voice whispers in the darkness, and I realize I've spoken my thoughts aloud. "I am here, Lyana. You can do this. You took an arrow for me," he says. "This is nothing compared to that."

I nod. "All right. Let's keep going."

I focus on my breathing as I force myself to move, one hand in front of the other as we crawl through the tunnel. To my surprise, it gets easier as we go.

"Are we almost there?"

Caelen hesitates a beat before he responds. "I… do not know."

A nervous chuckle escapes me. "You could have lied to make me feel better, you know."

"I thought you would appreciate honesty from your mate," he teases lightly. "You were angry at me for lying about the spiders, were you not?"

A faint smile curls my lips. "Normally, an honest husband is a good thing. But… not in this case, I think."

He's silent a moment. "Then… we are almost there."

I burst out laughing at his joke. "Too late. You already told me the truth; you cannot take it back now."

"I suppose not," he says, and I can hear the smile in his voice. "But we will be through it soon enough. I doubt your Dwarvish friend would have sent us this way if the pass were impossible."

A grin tugs at my lips. "Bran would be shocked to hear how much faith you have in him. I can hardly wait to tell him about it."

"Perhaps you best keep it to yourself. Dwarves are already full of themselves as it is."

"And I've heard the same of the Elves," I joke.

He scoffs. "Then, you've been misinformed."

I laugh again, the sound echoing loudly in the enclosed space. I stop abruptly and lower my voice. "Sorry. I did not mean to be so loud."

"It is all right," he replies. "I quite like the sound of your laughter."

Happiness blooms in my chest as I follow him through the darkness.

When we finally reach the other side, soft light spills in from an opening in the ceiling. It's not much, but I can at least see Caelen much better now. We stand and I tip my head up toward the light, relishing the cavernous space around us.

"We should rest a bit and eat something," he says. "We still have a long journey ahead of us, I'm afraid."

"All right."

Together, we sit side by side as we eat some of the bread and cheese from our packs. I shiver slightly and Caelen pulls out the bedroll and wraps it around me. "What about you?" I ask. "Are you not cold?"

"It is… not unbearable," he replies.

I lift the corner and drape it over his shoulder, wrapping it around us both. "Is that better?"

He flashes a handsome smile that makes my heart flutter. "Yes, it is. Thank you."

I lean into Caelen, eagerly soaking up the warmth radiating from his body. "Thank you for helping me earlier."

"Of course." His gaze sweeps to mine. "Have you always had a fear of enclosed spaces?"

"I fell down a well when I was younger. Arthur and I were playing with Bran and his brother Rob. They said it was a wishing well. I leaned over the edge to make a wish, and fell in." I shudder, and Caelen tightens his arm around me. "I was trapped for several hours before they got me out."

"That had to have been terrible."

"It was. And it's made me afraid ever since. But I realized something earlier."

"What was it?"

"If I am to regain my throne and rule Eryadon, I cannot afford to be afraid anymore." I swallow against the lump in my throat. "I am the last of my family. I am alone now." The words settle in my chest like a heavy stone. "I have to be brave."

He cups my chin, tipping my head up to his. "You are not alone, Lyana."

His gaze travels over my face like a gentle caress. I could so easily lose myself in his eyes. Caelen is not at all what I expected of a High Elf. He is warm, and kind, and caring. But it is not just that. Something about him draws me in.

I reach up and cup his cheek. I brush my thumb lightly across his full, lower lip. Maybe it is my recent fear that makes me so bold as to touch him in this way, or perhaps it is something else.

My heart pounds, and my entire body thrums with anticipation as he leans in close. The soft mint of his breath washes over my skin a moment before he closes the small gap between us. His lips brush against mine in a tender kiss.

He pulls back just enough to skim the tip of his nose alongside my own. He runs his fingers through my hair and cups the back of my head, pressing his lips again to mine in a tentative kiss, gentle and exploring. His masculine scent—cinnamon and spice—surrounds me.

His hands slide around my waist, pulling me close as he traces his tongue along the seam of my lips, asking for entrance.

I gasp, and his tongue finds mine, lightly stroking against it. Fire sparks deep within and our kiss becomes more urgent. He buries his hand in my hair, gripping the long strands to angle my face up to his as he claims my mouth with his lips and his tongue.

The soft scraping of stone echoes nearby, startling us both, and we pull away.

"What was that?"

A low growl rises in his throat as he scans the dark tunnel ahead. "Do not worry. I have warned them away."

"Them?" I ask, my voice nearly a squeak. "As in… more than one?"

He arches a brow. "Do you really wish to know?"

His question gives me pause. "Will whatever they are leave us alone?"

He nods.

"That's good enough for me, then."

He stands and extends his hand, pulling me up beside him. "There are more of them coming, however. We should go."

His words send a small shiver down my spine, but I force myself to push down my fear.

With my hand in his, we continue on through the darkness. He says nothing of our kiss and neither do I, but my mind keeps returning to the memory of his lips upon mine.

I should not have kissed him. We have already agreed to annul our marriage. He does not want a human wife.

And yet... he did not pull away until we were interrupted. Maybe he feels something for me, just as I do for him.

Or perhaps he regrets it, and that's why he does not mention it.

I feel so foolish for having kissed him when he probably does not even want me.

I want to ask him about this, but each time I open my mouth the words die in my throat. I'm not even sure where to begin.

But as we continue, I realize that we have far greater problems than this. We need to focus on surviving, not on analyzing emotions and feelings that may or may not be returned.

I force myself to push down my emotions. I'm in danger of losing my heart to this man, and that is something I do not want to risk. But as I glance at Caelen, I realize that it's already too late. I'm falling for him. And now, I can only hope that he somehow feels the same.

CHAPTER 28

CAELEN

I t has been a long day by the time we reach the tunnel's exit. The corridor is so small and narrow we've spent much of the day crawling on our hands and knees.

My mind keeps returning to our kiss. Even now, I miss the press of her soft lips against mine. She has said nothing about it since it happened, and I worry that perhaps she may regret it now.

Or maybe her mind was simply occupied with moving through the cave. I'm in awe of the amount of trust she has in me. She could see nothing through most of our journey, and relied upon me completely to guide her.

Light filters into the cavern up ahead as we make our way toward the cave mouth. With her hand still in mine, we walk toward it. The moment we reach the outside, I'm reluctant to let go of her hand, but there is no reason to hold onto her now that we're out in the light, and she can see clearly.

Lyana tilts her head up, and spreads her arms wide as if in a friendly greeting to the setting sun.

I stare at her, completely transfixed as the golden light surrounds and envelops her. She truly is the most beautiful woman I have ever seen.

Fierce possessiveness fills me as I observe her. When we married, I never expected to feel like this. To look upon her and ache with want to touch her petal-soft skin. To have to fight the urge to gather her in my arms and hold her close.

A cool breeze blows through her long, black hair. I long to run my fingers through the silken strands, gripping them firmly and tipping her head up to expose the long column of her neck.

According to her, the human vows we made were not binding, but as my gaze darts to the pulsing artery along her neck, I long more than anything to bind her to me in the ways of my people. Something dark and primal unfurls from deep within, demanding that I sink my fangs into her sensitive flesh and claim her as my true mate.

She turns to me. Her luminous golden-brown eyes search mine and I am completely lost in their depths. "Thank you," she murmurs. "For helping me through the cave."

Unable to speak, I dip my chin. My gaze travels over her face. I wonder if she would accept my dark kiss, or if it would scare her.

She seemed terrified of the prospect of the Wild Hunt when Bran mentioned it to her.

My gaze drops to her soft, full lips. I long to kiss her again, but I do not know if she wants this.

As much as I want to speak to her about what happened, I do not know how.

I realize I am staring at her when her cheeks flush bright red and she lowers her eyes from me.

Perhaps it is as I feared and she regrets our kiss.

Sighing heavily, I force my gaze from hers and scan the forest. We must focus on finding safety and shelter. I am certain Fredrik and the queen will not have given up their search for her.

The wind carries a faint hint of the crisp, saline scent of the ocean. We cannot be very far from Solwyck and the Northern Sea that borders its lands.

Beyond that, lies my kingdom—Rivenyl. But between here and there, I know that my kind are not well liked. I only pray we do not run into any trouble along the way.

CHAPTER 29

LYANA

After crawling through the tunnel most of the day, my clothing is completely wrinkled. I smooth my hand down my tunic to straighten the fabric, trying my best to appear unfazed when I am anything but.

I shouldn't have kissed him. How could I be so foolish to think he'd ever want me. Why *would he* want a human? I'm sure that I'm nothing compared to the beauty of an Elvish woman.

Studying Caelen, I note how handsome he is, even dressed in the Dwarvish clothing.

Dwarves are similar in height to humans but more sturdily built. With broad shoulders and chests and thick cords of muscles on their arms and legs, it is easy to tell them apart from humans.

However, as my gaze travels over Caelen, I cannot help but notice how much taller he is than they are. The hem of the pants they lent him barely reaches mid-calf, and the cloth is oddly fitted over his form. He is not a small man by any means. His broad shoulders taper to a narrow waist, and his body is lean and muscular. When I clung to him, in the cave, I noticed just how solidly built he is—not an ounce of fat on him.

My body warms at the memory of our kiss. I turn to regard the forest in front of us, forcing myself to focus. "How far do you think we are from the coast of Solwyck?"

His nostrils flare as he scents the wind. "The smell of the sea and the ash is faint here. Perhaps a day's travel before we reach the border between Eryadon and Solwyck. Then, another day beyond that to Rivenyl." He turns to me. "We should get as far from here as possible in case any of Fredrik's people somehow learn of this tunnel."

Worry fills me as I think on Bran and the Dwarves, hoping they're all right. "Do you think Fredrik and his army left the Dwarves alone to their mountain after we left?"

"The Dwarves are skilled in illusory magic. I am certain the decoy worked to lure Fredrik's people away."

"I hope so," I murmur. I look toward the horizon. "Let's get going."

As we traverse the woods, his eyes continually scan our surroundings as if searching for danger. Something moves in the forest ahead, and he pauses. Fear ripples up my spine when he grasps my forearm and pulls me behind him.

"What is it?" I ask, my voice barely a whisper.

"A Wolf shifter," he replies in a voice so low I almost miss it. "If I tell you to run, do not hesitate."

I draw the dagger from my belt. After everything he has done for me, there's no way I'd leave him behind. "I won't leave you."

His deadly fangs and claws emerge as he stares straight ahead. "Show yourself, Wolf," he snarls.

My heart pounds when a man steps from the shadows. His glowing, green eyes study us with a menacing glare, baring two rows of gleaming white fangs in a feral grin. "Since when does a High Elf protect a human?"

Caelen growls low in his throat. "Who are you?"

"A hunter," he says in a low and sinister voice. "The queen sent me to kill the princess and bring back her heart."

Fear twists deep in my gut. I hold the knife out before me as the Wolf's gaze remains locked on mine.

"You will die before you touch her," Caelen snarls.

"Calm yourself, Prince Caelen," the Wolf growls. "I have no intention of killing your mate."

"Then why are you here?" Caelen grinds out.

The Wolf turns his attention back to me. I observe in shock as he drops to one knee and bows low. "My name is Malak, and I have come to warn you, Princess. I am not the only hunter the queen has sent. Another follows close behind me. His name is Kalov, and he is one of our best trackers."

I study him warily. "Why should I trust you?"

He lifts his head. "Your brother, Arthur, saved my life once. I swore a blood oath to him in return. Because your brother is gone, my oath now extends to you."

"Malak." Caelen growls low. "I knew I recognized your name. You are a prince of Winterhold—second in line for the throne. Why would you betray your own brother, Prince Fredrik?"

I inhale sharply.

Malak narrows his eyes. "If you know who I am, then you have undoubtedly heard my story."

Caelen dips his chin in a subtle nod.

"I swear it on my beloved Luna, that what I speak is truth. I came here to warn you," he replies solemnly. "And may the gods strike me down if I am lying."

Caelen relaxes his stance. He studies Malak a moment before he takes my hand and pulls me to his side. "Tell us how to avoid this hunter—Kalov."

"He is about a half day's journey behind you," Malak answers. "When I heard Fredrik give the order to hunt you down, I knew you'd be heading straight for Rivenyl."

"How did you know where to find us?" I ask.

"I didn't. I prayed to the old gods. They whispered your location to me through the earth and the trees."

I have never heard of the old gods speaking to someone this way.

"I do not expect your kind to understand the ways of the old gods," he says, probably reading the doubt in my expression. "The human race has forgotten many things from its past. Not all of my kin remember them either. *I* am one of the few who remain."

"You'd betray Fredrik, your own brother, for us?" I ask.

He stands. "Yes. I have more reason than the blood oath I made to your brother, to help you. Fredrik and my father threatened to kill she whom I adore above all else. And I would see Fredrik and my father's reign end, not grow stronger by conquering Eryadon."

"Eryadon is already conquered," I tell him, the words like bitter acid deep in my gut. "My father is dead and my step-mother now sits on the throne beside your brother."

He regards me soberly. "You are still alive, Princess. Not all hope is lost." He pauses. "That is why they hunt you."

I tip my chin up to meet his eyes evenly. "And how do you plan to help us?"

"Give me an item of your clothing, Princess." He looks to Caelen. "And trade clothes with me, Prince Caelen. You will not reach Solwyck before tomorrow, and you are vulnerable until then."

"Why do you want our things?" I ask.

"I will take them in the opposite direction from here. I'll travel toward the Fae Kingdom of Anara, leading Kalov away from you by laying a false trail with your scent. It is well-known that Anara and Rivenyl are allies, so I believe he will follow it." His gaze shifts to Caelen. "What say you? Will you trust me?"

Caelen darts a glance at me, and dips his chin in a subtle nod.

Malak's story sounds convincing, and the fact that Caelen is inclined to trust him is enough for me to agree. Caelen has done nothing but look out for me from the beginning. He would not drop his guard for no reason. "We will."

"We must hurry," Malak says, already removing his tunic.

I turn as they both change quickly and I remove my bra. It's the only item I can spare. I'm too cold to part with anything else. Caelen wrinkles his nose once he's redressed, and Malak snorts out a laugh. "The feeling is mutual. I dislike the stench of Elf as much as you dislike the smell of Wolf, Prince Caelen."

Caelen narrows his eyes, but I note his lips quirk up slightly at the edges.

Malak arches a brow as I hand him my bra. His nostrils flare and he gives Caelen a wolfish grin. "I'd heard yours was a marriage of politics only. So why does this item smell so much like High Elf?"

My cheeks heat in embarrassment and Caelen growls low in his throat, leveling a dark glare at him.

"Relax," Malak says, raising his hands up in mock surrender. "I am only teasing you, Elf. I know what it is to love a human."

Caelen straightens and extends his arm. Malak takes it, each of them gripping the other's forearm. "We will not forget this."

Malak dips his chin in a firm nod and turns his attention back to me. "I'll need your bedroll as well," he says, holding out his own. "Here. Take mine."

As we make the exchange, Caelen blows a sharp huff of

air out his nose as if the scent is offensive. I, on the other hand, can smell nothing.

"You should wear this as well." Malak hands me a cloak.

For all Caelen claims it is the Fae who are dramatic, he wrinkles his nose again in disgust.

Malak continues. "This cloak is enchanted to conceal your form. It will hide your true appearance."

I extend my hand, and he takes it. "Thank you for your kindness."

His green eyes pierce mine. "Prince Arthur was a great man and an even greater warrior. I am honored to have known him and I am sorry that he has gone from this world."

I swallow against the lump in my throat at the memory of my brother.

"What will happen to you if Fredrik finds out that you helped me?"

"That is not for you to worry over, Princess. You are the last of your great and noble line. Your job is to stay alive."

Caelen dips his chin in parting. "Thank you, Malak."

With another bow, Malak races off through the woods, leaving us alone again.

Caelen makes sure the cloak is firmly wrapped around me. He removes his belt and cinches it around my waist to hold it in place.

There's something so caring and intimate about the way he takes extra care to make sure I'm completely covered by the cloak. Caelen leans in, and my skin prickles in awareness as his nose skims across my sensitive flesh as he scents me.

Malak's words resurface in my mind. He told Caelen that he knew what it was to love a human, and I wonder, for the first time, if perhaps my feelings for Caelen are not completely one-sided, like I'd believed.

When he pulls back, he flashes a charming smile. "All

good," he says. "I can barely detect your scent over the stench of the wolf."

I rub the back of my neck. "And… that's good, I hope."

He nods. "Very." He reaches out for my hand, and I slide my palm into his. "Let's go."

CHAPTER 30

CAELEN

As we travel, Lyana's steps begin to falter. "Do you want to stop and rest for a bit?"

She straightens, and tips up her chin in determination. "No. We should keep going as long as we can."

"Would you like me to carry you?" I offer. Before she can answer, I add, "Your weight is very slight; it would not be a burden to me."

She gives me a faint smile. "Thank you, Caelen, but I can walk."

I study her out of the corner of my eye as we continue. It is easy to see that she is exhausted, but she refuses to stop. Her strength of will is as strong as that of a High Elf.

The sun dips toward the earth, and shadows lengthen through the trees. I am not sure how much further we must trek, but her fatigue is weighing her down. Nevertheless, her face is a mask of resolve.

I turn my attention back to the surrounding forest. The

last of the sun's golden rays spread out across the land, reminding me that night will soon be upon us.

We need to find somewhere to rest, preferably not out in the open. I mutter a curse under my breath. If not for the treaty with Eryadon, I'd be able to use my magic to conceal us from enemy eyes while we slept.

Because I cannot, I must choose where we will rest very carefully. Malak said it is not just any Wolf that hunts us; it is one of their best trackers.

Anger roils deep inside me. I will end anyone who dares try to harm my mate.

And yet… she is not mine. Not truly.

We kissed, but she has made it clear she does not desire me as her husband. She spoke sacred vows but claims they were mere words. I do not understand. My people never make promises lightly, but it seems hers do.

"Malak mentioned someone named Luna." Lyana's voice rips me from my thoughts. "Who is she?"

"I have heard she is his beloved, although I was surprised he actually admitted it."

"Why?"

"She is human."

"And… that's a bad thing?"

"Not necessarily bad," I answer. "Just… difficult."

Lyana turns to me. "I do not understand."

"It is a risk for any of my kind to fall in love with yours."

"Your kind? You're a High Elf, not a Wolf shifter."

"Otherworldly beings: Elves, Wolves, Fae, Dragons, Mer, and such," I explain. "When we love, it is complete and all-consuming. An irrevocable truth that resonates deep in our soul, changing the very core of our being. Once our heart is given to another, there is no returning to what we once were. And never will we be whole without the one to whom we have pledged our devotion."

"Are you saying that once your kind loves someone, it's forever?" she asks.

When she promised me her love with her human vows, I believed that she meant it. My heart swelled with hope at the prospect of not just a partnership, but a marriage of love.

I turn and meet her lovely, golden-brown eyes steadily. "Yes."

CHAPTER 31

LYANA

His green eyes search mine full of an emotion that I cannot quite discern. Could it be that he has feelings for me, like I do him? Or does he regret our kiss?

"Caelen, when we kissed, I—"

"You regret it," he cuts me off. "I am sorry. I did not mean to take advantage of you while you were afraid and vulnerable."

"Take advantage?" I ask, my voice rising in pitch. "What are you talking about? *I* kissed you back."

"Yes, but you were in a vulnerable state," he says. "I should not have—"

I press a finger to his lips to silence him. "Caelen, I do not—"

I stop short as a piercing howl echoes through the forest behind us.

Caelen's eyes widen.

"Is it a Wolf shifter or simply a wolf?"

JESSICA GRAYSON & ARIA WINTER

"I cannot tell," he replies. "We should keep moving. We must get as far away from here as possible and find shelter for the night."

"I agree."

We move deeper into the woods. Shadows dance at the edge of my vision, filling me with concern.

When I glance at Caelen, however, and notice that he appears unconcerned about them, it helps calm some of my fears. We have not heard the wolf's howl again, but the thought that the hunter could be tracking us worries me.

This area appears rather wild compared to the forest near the castle. Long, wiry branches pull at our clothing like skeletal hands, as if trying to ensnare us. The sounds of nocturnal creatures and insects fill the air.

Reflective eyes watch us warily as we pass, but none approach. The screech of an owl nearby startles me and I press myself closer to Caelen, knowing that his eyes can see much better than mine in the darkness.

He continually scans for any danger, as I remain silent beside him. I dare not disturb him with idle conversation. Especially knowing that the hunter could be closing in on our position even now.

The sound of rushing water reaches my ears and sparks hope in my chest. I used to study maps of Eryadon when I was a child. The border between our kingdom and Solwyck's was the Merlyan River. I turn to Caelen. "If my memory of this area is correct, there's a wide river up ahead. If we can find a way to cross, it should make it harder for the hunter to track us."

He nods. "Let us hurry then. We can find somewhere to shelter on the opposite side."

CHAPTER 32

CAELEN

We make our way to the water's edge, but I am discouraged to realize just how wide the river is and how swift the current. I do not know its depth, but I know it will not be easy to cross, especially for Lyana, who is much shorter and not as strong as a High Elf.

Her eyes are wide as she studies the turbulent water, no doubt assessing the fast-moving torrent with a healthy dose of cautionary fear.

"Can you swim?"

"Yes." As if reading my concern, she adds, "We have to do this, Caelen. We do not have a choice."

Panic tightens my chest at the thought of her being swept away. "I'm going to tie you to me, like we did when we went through the narrow part of the tunnels."

"No," she states firmly. "It's too dangerous. If I were to get swept away, I'd pull you down with me. I don't want you to drown."

"I am a High Elf," I counter. "I am stronger than you. The chances of us both drowning while tied together are—"

"More than I'm willing to risk," she interrupts. She sets her jaw and looks back at the water. "Let's go."

She approaches the riverbank, staring transfixed at the current. "It's too strong, Lyana. We should travel further down and find another way."

"All right," she replies. "We'll—"

A howl echoes through the forest behind us. I spin toward it, scenting the air, hoping it is merely a wolf and not a shifter. I clench my jaw as my nostrils fill with a familiar stench. "Wolf shifter," I curse under my breath. "We'll have to cross here. We do not have a choice."

I take off my pack and quickly rummage through it for my rope. As soon as I find it, I stand and loop it around Lyana's waist.

"Caelen, no!"

My eyes snap to hers. "Forgive me, *my wife*," I emphasize the title. "But I do not care what you say right now. What kind of husband would not do everything he could to keep his mate alive?"

I tie the rope in a firm knot around her waist and then secure the other end to myself. "Give me your pack," I demand, my tone a bit harsher than I'd intended, but we do not have time to argue. "I'm going to strap them both to my front."

She does as I ask, and I study the water once more before turning my attention back to her. "I'm going to carry you on my back, but you must hold on, no matter what. Can you do this?"

Her eyes search mine. "Yes."

"All right. Climb on." I start to turn my back to her, but her hand on my forearm halts me.

"Caelen, wait."

"What is it?"

She stretches up on her toes until her face is almost level with my own. She cups my cheek. "I just want you to know, in case anything happens to me, that I'm glad it was you."

I start to ask what she means but stop abruptly. Her luminous golden-brown eyes search mine and I am lost in their depths. She leans in and presses a tender kiss to my lips.

It is all too brief, and when she pulls back, I am reluctant to let her go. I twine my arms around her waist, and drop my forehead gently to hers.

"I know you did not want this marriage, Caelen, but you have been a wonderful husband. And I am glad that out of everyone I could have ended up with, that it was you."

She still believes I do not desire this marriage. In truth, I did not. Not at first. But now, everything is different. I've fallen in love with her. A human. A woman who has possessed me: body, mind, heart, and soul. "Lyana, I—"

Another howl pierces the air and worry floods my veins. There is no time to tell her all that I want and need to say. My words and feelings will have to wait. I must get my mate to safety. "Whatever happens, do not let go of me."

She nods.

I turn and she climbs onto my back, coiling her legs around my torso and her arms tight around my neck. Drawing in a deep breath, I start toward the river.

The cool water runs over my feet and ankles and then up my legs as I wade in. The current is dangerously swift as it pulls at my form, trying to drag me into its ice-cold depths.

We're not even halfway across and it's already up to my waist. The instinct to lock my arms around Lyana's lithe form is strong, but I need my arms free to keep my balance as we cross.

The turbulent water threatens to sweep us away, but I fight with everything inside me to keep moving forward.

Another piercing howl makes the hair rise on the back of my neck; this one far too close for my liking. The silver moon shines down from above, casting an eerie glow across the roiling water.

I take another step and the river bottom drops off, plunging us into the icy water. The torrent sweeps us up and drags us down the river. My limbs burn with exertion as I fight against the current, struggling to keep us above the surface.

Panic fills me as Lyana's hold begins to loosen.

"Do not let go!" I yell over my shoulder.

"I'm—" Her words are swallowed by the water as she loses her grip and the current rips her away. The sharp tug, a moment later, on the rope between us jerks my entire body, pulling me under. My arms and legs flail wildly as I go tumbling along the riverbed, grasping for anything to hold onto.

My hand slams against something solid and I grip it tightly, pulling myself up. The sharp tug of the rope threatens to drag me back under, but I manage to break through the surface.

Gasping for air, I scan downstream for Lyana, but see nothing. "Lyana!"

I brace myself against a partially submerged branch and pull at the rope, but it's no use. The current is too strong.

Fear stops my heart.

I will die or I will save her, but I will not let her go.

I release my grip on the branch and allow the water to take me, praying that it leads me to my mate.

Hand over hand, I haul on the rope as I'm swept along, the resistance telling me she's still on the other end. When I bump against her, I wrap one arm solidly around her form, and push off the riverbed toward the surface.

As soon as we break through, I stroke with all my might.

Her body is limp even as I hold her head above the surface, and panic threatens to consume me, but I force myself to press on. I have to get us out of the water. My muscles ache in protest as I pump my arms and legs, desperate to reach the shore.

Up ahead I spot a low-hanging branch that extends out from the shore, and into the river. The current carries us toward it and I grab hold.

With one arm banded around Lyana and the other on the branch, I manage to wrap my legs around it and pull us toward the shore. After what feels like forever, my feet find purchase on the riverbed, and I force my body to keep going despite my exhaustion.

I drag us up onto the riverbank, and roll her onto her back.

Her eyes are closed. A blue tinge colors her normally pink lips and she lies with a stillness that stops my heart. "Lyana!" I cry out, watching for her eyes to flutter and open.

But she remains still. Warm tears escape my lashes. "No! I won't lose you!"

Remembering the time that my sister nearly drowned, I recall how Ruvaen saved her. I place my hands on Lyana's chest and begin the compressions that I once watched him perform.

Her eyes fly open and I turn her onto her side as she coughs the water up from her lungs.

She draws in great gulping breaths. I pull her into my arms, sending a silent prayer to the old gods for sparing her life.

Gently, I brush the hair back from her face as I study her. Extending my fangs, I bite my wrist to draw blood and then place it over her mouth, sharing some of my life force to help her.

She tries to turn her head, but I protest. "Please. You need strength. You must drink."

She stops fighting and does as I ask.

When I pull my wrist away, I am glad to see her color beginning to return, but she is still shivering uncontrollably. If I do not get her warm, she could freeze to death.

I push myself up and force my aching body to stand. I loop the packs over my shoulder and gather her in my arms and trudge toward the forest.

I check over my shoulder, satisfied that we don't appear to have been followed. I look down at Lyana, her teeth chattering as she folds herself into my chest, seeking warmth.

I find a large grouping of boulders and move to the far side, away from the river. I carefully set Lyana on the ground, propping her up against one as I dig through the pack, searching for anything to keep her warm.

Everything is completely soaked and unusable. We need fire. But I—

I stop as the mere thought makes a small flame flicker in my upturned palm. I smile in relief. "We are beyond Eryadon's borders."

I close my eyes, summoning the last of my strength and filling my veins with the familiar energy of my magic. It flows through my body, crackling between my fingers like lightning.

Lyana's eyes are wide as I speak the words of enchantment to create a barrier, concealing us from enemy eyes. In my weakened state, my body sways as I seal it in place. I conjure fire to warm us, the roaring flames providing warmth and light.

As the magic flows through me, my strength begins to wane. My hands shake as I lower them to my sides. This is all I can manage right now, but it should be enough.

I move to Lyana. "Forgive me," I say as I begin to strip her of her clothes. "You will freeze if you stay in these."

Unable to speak through her chattering teeth, she nods. I remove mine as well, leaving us only in our underwear.

I avert my eyes, not wanting to look upon her nearly naked form because I know it makes her uncomfortable in even the best of times. But I also know we have no time for modesty as I pull her back against my chest, wrapping her in my body as I curl protectively around her.

I tuck her feet between my calves, angling us as close to the fire as I can. I loop my arm around her waist, locking her in place and molding her to me. She snuggles even further against my chest, and I'm pleased when her shivering begins to ease.

She tips her face up to me, her luminous golden-brown eyes searching my own. "You could have died, Caelen," she whispers. "Why did you risk your life for me?"

"Because you are mine." The words leave my lips, full of conviction because it is true.

She *is* mine.

Mine to love. Mine to protect. Mine to cherish. She is my mate and I am hers.

"Sleep, Lyana." I speak softly. "You must rest."

As her eyes close, I gently brush the hair back from her face and study her lovely features, thankful that she lives. "*Ashal'veh*," I whisper the ancient Elvish words for *I love you*.

Closing my eyes, I allow myself to fall into oblivion.

CHAPTER 33

LYANA

W hen I wake, it's still dark. The soft light of the fire casts flickering shadows across the ground before me. I'm cocooned by warmth. I shift slightly and something tightens around my waist.

I glance down beneath the blanket, and notice Caelen's arm. With my back pressed against his front and his knees tucked up under mine, his powerful frame is coiled protectively around my own.

His breath is warm in my ear as he whispers, "You are awake."

My heart hammers and my breath catches in my throat as my entire body hums in response to his. "Yes," I barely manage. It occurs to me that I'm only in my underwear. My cheeks burn.

He shifts slightly, and a shiver runs through me; not one of cold, but one of pleasure. He disentangles his limbs and stands. I instinctively band an arm across my chest and pull the blanket over my shoulders.

He's only partially dressed as well. The firelight accentuates his broad shoulders and the rippling muscles of his chest and abdomen as he retrieves my cloak from a nearby rock.

He holds it out to me, careful to avert his eyes from my nearly naked form. "It should be dry now."

"Thank you."

I cover myself with the cloak while he checks the rest of our clothes. "Everything else is still a bit wet, but it should be ready shortly," he says.

I pull the cloak around my shoulders, both for warmth and to hide my nearly naked form.

Caelen returns to my side and sits down next to me. He's not shivering, but the breeze is still rather cold. "Here." I lift the end of my blanket and wrap it around his shoulder so it enfolds us both.

"I am fine. You need this more than I do."

"I insist. It's cold out here."

A smirk twists his lips. "Perhaps for a fragile human, but for an Elf—"

"Before you continue, I think it's best you not forget that this *fragile human* is your wife," I tease.

His expression sobers. "How could I?" Something—an emotion—flashes behind his eyes as they search mine, but it's gone too quickly for me to identify. He cups my chin and tips my face up to his.

His piercing gaze studies me a moment before he gently drops his forehead against mine. "You nearly drowned."

"But, I didn't."

Clenching his jaw, he lowers his gaze.

I take his hand. "Caelen, what's wrong?"

He shakes his head softly. "You are human... and I wish you were not."

I jerk away, instantly offended. "Well, I'm sorry to disappoint you, Caelen, but I cannot change what I am."

His eyes flick back up to mine. "You do not understand."

"What don't I understand?" I snap.

"Your human body… it is not nearly as strong as that of a High Elf, and—"

"Well, don't worry, once our marriage is annulled, you can marry one of your own kind instead."

"I do not want anyone else," he fires back. "I could have lost you, Lyana. Your human body is fragile compared to my people and it terrifies me."

"Why?"

"Because I cannot bear the thought of losing you." The words leave his lips in a rush. "You could have died, Lyana."

"But I didn't." I reach out and cup his cheek. "I'm still here, Caelen. You saved me."

He closes his eyes, tilting his face into my hand as if relishing the touch of my skin upon his own. When he opens them again, his gaze holds mine, full of sadness and longing.

"*Ashal'veh*," he whispers, and although I do not know what these words mean, I understand their meaning as his green eyes stare deep into mine, full of love and devotion. These are words that need no translation to be understood. They resonate deep in my soul.

He clasps the back of my head and seals his mouth over mine in a searing kiss, stealing the breath from my lungs. His fingers tangle in my hair, gripping the long strands and tipping my head back as his tongue strokes against my own, both demanding and giving all at once.

My heart beats wildly in my chest; I'm breathless and panting as he takes complete control of our kiss, devouring me with his lips and his tongue.

"Gods help me," he breathes between kisses. "I love you."

Happiness blooms in my chest as I smile against his lips. "You love me?"

"More than anything." He pulls back just enough to cup

173

my chin, brushing the soft pad of his thumb across my cheek as he studies me intently.

"Even though I'm human?" I ask, just to be sure.

His gaze travels over my face like a gentle caress as he takes my hand and entwines our fingers. "I want no one but you, my beautiful human wife."

A beaming smile curves my mouth. "And I want no one but you, my handsome High Elf husband."

My words unleash something inside him, and Caelen crushes his lips to mine in a branding kiss. He pulls me into his lap, my thighs straddling his hips. My cloak falls away. Only his soft knit pants and the soft silken scrap of material between my thighs separates us.

His hands move over my skin, possessive and claiming, as he pulls me close, molding my body to his.

I trace my fingers over the pointed tip of his left ear and he growls low in arousal. Without warning, he twists and lays me on the ground, pinning me beneath him.

A soft moan escapes me as he rolls his hips against mine and his hardened length presses insistently against my center.

Pleasure pools deep inside me as I run my hands down the defined muscles of his back, feeling the flex and give of his powerful form as he moves over me.

He rips his mouth from mine and kisses a heated trail along my jaw and down my neck to my breasts.

"Caelen," I breathe as I arch up against him. I dig my nails into his muscular shoulders as his tongue traces over the gentle slope of one breast and closes his mouth over the sensitive peak.

He begins a gentle suction, sending ripples of pleasure straight down to my core.

Overwhelming sensations moves through me as he laves

at my breast. I run my fingers through his hair as he turns his attention to the other one.

He lifts his head. His nostrils flare and his eyes meet mine, full of desire and hunger. "I can scent your need, my mate. I long to taste you on my tongue."

Heat flares my cheeks at his bold words.

He dips his hand beneath the silken band of fabric at my hips and gently pulls it down and off my body. The tips of his fingers skim up my legs and slowly part my thighs, baring me to his gaze.

His green eyes stare deep into mine as he dips one finger between my already slick folds. A low moan escapes my lips when he reaches the small pearl of flesh at the top, and I arch into his hand.

He concentrates his attention on this sensitive bundle of nerves, studying my reactions to his touch.

My heart beats wildly in my chest. It's too much and not enough all at once. My legs tremble as if my body cannot decide whether to pull him closer or push him away as pleasure builds deep within.

"Caelen, please," I breathe, not even sure what I'm asking for.

He dips his head between my thighs, and I cry out as he replaces his finger with his tongue. A deep rumble emerges from his throat and the vibration moves straight through me. My entire body tenses, as pleasure coils tightly within. "Caelen," I barely manage. "I've never felt anything like this."

He lifts his head, his gaze full of fire and possession. He brushes his thumb over the softly hooded flesh, concentrating on the touches that make me arch into his hand.

Remembering how sensitive his ears are, I reach down and run my fingers over the pointed tips.

He growls and moves back up my body, capturing my

mouth with his own as he continues to tease his fingers through my folds. "Elf ears are sensitive, Lyana. If you do not stop, I will be unable to resist claiming you," he rasps.

"I'm already yours," I whisper against his lips.

CHAPTER 34

CAELEN

Dark and primal instinct rises from deep within at her words. My *stav* is hard and painfully erect with desire to join my body to hers. I long to mark her and seal her to me in the ancient blood bond of my people.

She digs her nails into my back as she arches against me. I grasp her chin, forcing her gaze to mine. I want to watch her as she finds her release.

Her golden-brown eyes stare deep into mine. She moans softly as I brush my thumb over the softly hooded flesh between her thighs. This spot is sensitive for her, more so than anywhere else on her body.

"Caelen," she pants. "This feels… I don't know what I'm supposed to—"

"Let go," I whisper.

Her head falls back, her lips part, and she cries out my name as she shatters.

A growl of arousal vibrates my chest. My eyes fall on the

artery along her neck, and my fangs extend, yearning to claim her, and give her my dark kiss.

She inhales sharply and the acrid tang of fear thickens the air.

I quickly pull back, retracting my fangs. "Forgive me."

She lies completely still, her eyes wide as they search mine. "It is true, then," she says, her voice barely more than a whisper.

"What is?"

"You mark your mates and seal them to you with blood."

"It is the blood bond, yes. We call it the dark kiss."

I look away. I cannot bear the sight of fear in her eyes as she regards me. "I… did not mean to frighten you, Lyana. Please, forgive me."

She takes my hand, threading her fingers through mine as she smiles faintly. "It is all right," she says, although I note the slight tremble of her voice. "I was simply… startled. That's all."

Lyana moves close to me, wrapping her arms around my waist and tucking herself against my chest.

The acrid scent of her fear still lingers in the air, burning my lungs with each inhalation. I hate that I am the reason she was afraid, when I want only to protect her… to cherish, and love her.

Cautiously, I curl my arms around her smaller form and run my fingers through her long dark hair. Her skin is petal soft and her entire body so pliant and giving. She is fragile, my mate, and I can hardly bear the thought of hurting her.

The ritual of the blood bond is not gentle. She deserves to be worshipped and taken tenderly. For the first time in my life, I wish I were human. How can I bond her to me when I know it will hurt her? I saw the fear in her eyes and I've no wish to see it again.

"Caelen, I'm sorry," she whispers.

"You have nothing to apologize for. I understand." I hug her to my chest. "Rest, my Lyana. We must leave as soon as the sun is up."

Reluctantly, she nods and I listen as the sound of her breathing becomes soft and even.

My eyes trace gently over the delicate contours of her face, while she sleeps. Pain stabs through my heart like a sharpened blade.

She looked at me as if I were a monster. I hold her close, relishing the feel of her in my arms, and fearing this may be the last time she will ever allow me to touch her like this.

I did not intend to fall in love with Lyana, but I cannot undo what is done. If she decides she does not want me, I will have no choice but to accept her decision… even if it shatters my heart.

CHAPTER 35

LYANA

When I wake in the morning, I find Caelen has already packed our things. He gives me a folded cloth containing cheese and dried meat, but he keeps his gaze averted. Things are awkward between us, and I hate that I've caused this strained tension between us.

Why did I flinch when he bared his fangs to me? He was simply following Elvish customs, not trying to hurt me. We need to talk about what happened. I touch his shoulder, and his eyes snap up. "Caelen, I think we should—"

"We should be on our way," he interrupts. He studies the sky. Storm clouds gather overhead and thunder rumbles in the distance. "It is a long journey to Solwyck. We'll need to find a ship from there to reach my kingdom. It will be faster to travel by sea. Only then will we be safe."

I nod. He is right; we need to focus on reaching Solwyck. Princess Halla is a distant cousin on my mother's side. Although I have not seen her since we were children, I hope she will honor the blood ties between us and offer us aid. Surely, she will.

As we travel, Caelen offers several times to carry my pack, but I refuse. I do not want him to shoulder most of the burden.

"It is too heavy for you," he protests. "Please, allow me to—"

"I am stronger than you think."

He arches a brow. "Humans are not as physically strong as High Elves."

I clench my jaw. "I'm not some weak and pitiful creature." I lift my chin. "And despite what happened, I know you think I'm afraid of you, but I'm not, Caelen."

He tenses. "I could smell your fear."

"Yes, but that does not mean that—" I break off as a loud crack of thunder booms overhead. The skies open up and rain pours down in thick, heavy sheets.

I pull my hood up over my head, but it does little good. Caelen takes my hand. "We must find shelter."

He pulls me alongside him, moving so quickly I can barely keep up with his much longer legs. My foot snags on a root and I stumble, but he catches me, helping me regain my balance.

A cottage is just visible through the deluge in the distance. "Look!" I point toward it and Caelen snaps his head in that direction.

With no other choice, we head to the small building as I send a silent prayer that whoever is there will be welcoming and allow us to seek shelter within.

As we draw closer, I notice the cottage appears to be in a heavy state of disrepair. With broken windows and holes in the siding, surely it must be abandoned. The small, wooden fence surrounding it has seen better days. The gate squeaks on sagging hinges as Caelen pushes it open.

When we reach the front door, he knocks, but no one answers. Carefully, he tries the handle and then pushes it open, the heavy wooden door creaking as it moves. The entire space inside is dark and has only one small cot near the fireplace, a rickety table, four chairs, and a rocker across from the bed.

The floor is nothing more than bare earth. In a small kitchen area to one side, two rows of shelves flank the sink, cups and plates stacked haphazardly atop them. Cobwebs full of dust hang from the ceiling. Caelen brushes them aside as we make our way toward the fireplace.

He releases my hand and gestures to the grate. Closing his eyes, he speaks words of enchantment, lighting the hearth in the blink of an eye.

I smile and raise my hands out toward it, basking in the warmth. "Oh, thank goodness," I murmur. I remove my cloak and hang the sodden material on a small hook on the mantle. Caelen does the same with his.

Our travel packs are drenched, so we remove our bedrolls and place them close to the fire to dry. A musty blanket on the cot draws my attention and I shake it out, coughing as dust motes float through the air, while Caelen places two chairs before the hearth.

When I'm finished, I push the chairs close together and motion for him to sit. I wrap the blanket around our shoulders as we stare at the dancing flames.

I'm tired, but I'm not sure I can sleep. Not here anyway. Something about this place unnerves me. Despite its current state, something feels strange. As if perhaps its owner has merely stepped out for a moment but will return soon.

I turn to Caelen. "This place feels off, does it not?"

He nods, his eyes scanning the room, searching for danger. "We will leave here as soon as the rain stops."

"Agreed."

As we sit side by side, I consider the events from last night. We still haven't talked about it. I turn to him and place my hand atop his own. His green eyes snap up to mine. "Caelen, I—"

A loud knock on the door startles us both. Caelen jumps to his feet. I stand as well, but he motions for me to stay behind him as he nears the door.

It cracks open just a bit before he reaches it and he steps back, spreading his arms out to his sides as if to shield me from whatever approaches.

Rolling thunder booms overhead, rattling the windows and the plates on the shelf.

An old woman shuffles in, her back hunched and her head staring at the floor as water drips from her sodden clothes. She lifts a weary gaze to us as she pulls back the hood of her dark, tattered cloak. Her face splits into a smile, revealing several missing teeth. "Well, this is a pleasant surprise," she says cheerily. "Oh, it has been so long since I've had any visitors."

I move beside Caelen. "Forgive us." I bow slightly. "We sought shelter from the storm; we did not mean to intrude."

The old woman waves a dismissive hand. "It is no trouble, my dear. You are welcome to stay as long as you need." Her eyes flick to Caelen. "Both of you."

Gnarled fingers struggle to unfasten her cloak, so I rush forward and help her remove it. I hang it on the mantle to dry. "Thank you, my dear. That was very kind of you."

I flash a warm smile. "It's the least I can do for you allowing us to stay here." I glance at the kitchen. "Would you like me to start some tea?"

She shakes her head. "I'd be a poor host indeed if I had a guest wait upon me, now wouldn't I?"

Caelen stands beside me, his entire body alert, but he says nothing.

"Sit by the fire and warm yourselves," the old woman says. "I will make you both a nice cup of tea."

Caelen motions for me to take the seat furthest away from her, angling his chair so he can watch her covertly as she putters around in the kitchen.

"My name is Glenda," she says. "What is yours?"

I share a worried glance with Caelen before answering. "I am Lilly and this is my husband Callen."

Caelen's brow arches slightly. He's probably surprised at how quickly the false names spilled from my lips. Little does he know I already had them made up in my head after our meeting with Malak, prepared for a moment just like this.

A smile tips her mouth. "A High Elf and a human. I've not seen such a pairing in many years now."

Caelen takes my hand, squeezing it gently while his eyes remain trained upon her. His every muscle is tense, as if coiled and ready to spring into action if she so much as breathes wrong.

I do not understand his concern. She seems like a harmless, old woman. Even so, I trust him. And if his instincts are telling him something is off, I will not let my guard down either. I glance at the broken window, watching as the rain pours down heavily outside. Unfortunately, this storm doesn't appear to be letting up anytime soon.

The old woman hobbles over to us with two cups rattling in the saucers from her trembling hands. I jump up from my chair and move to help her. She smiles brightly at me. "Thank you, Lilly."

She sits beside us, turning to Caelen. "The Fae Prince of Anara has bound himself to a human as well, recently. And surely you've heard of the dragon and his human mate."

Caelen raises his brows. "A dragon and a human?"

"Aye," she replies.

"I've heard of this as well," I offer, knowing she speaks of the cursed dragon that lives at the edge of our kingdom, near the sea. Father was informed not long ago that the dragon had taken a village maiden as his bride. "I have heard she is happy with her dragon."

Glenda shivers, and I move to drape the blanket around her shoulders. She grasps my hand, patting it gently as she smiles. "You are most kind, dear girl." She narrows her eyes at Caelen, a grin tugging at her mouth as she wags a finger at him. "And you are most protective, dear boy, of your mate."

Caelen straightens but says nothing.

"You are wise to be this way," she says. "My sister wishes you both harm."

Without warning, Caelen shoots to his feet. He places himself directly between me and the old woman. A low growl vibrates in his chest as his nails lengthen into deadly claws. "What are you *really*, old woman?" he snarls. "Speak truth or I will end you."

She takes a sip of her tea and then sighs heavily. She waves a hand over her form and I gape as she transforms into a beautiful woman with pale lavender skin. Long purple hair falls around her shoulders in silken waves. Dressed in a long, green velvet robe, her amber, reptilian eyes study us both with a piercing gaze.

"Goblin," Caelen mutters, more to himself than to us. Magic sparks like electricity across the tips of his fingers. "If you dare try anything, I will end you."

She sighs again. "I suppose I might react the same if I were you, Prince Caelen, but I assure you, I mean neither of you any harm."

"Why lie about what you are then?" I ask.

She shrugs. "The easiest way to see into someone's heart is to observe how they treat those who are… lesser in some way." Her eyes meet mine evenly. "You, Princess Lyana, are pure of heart. And you, Prince Caelen, are firmly devoted to your bride." She pauses. "In return for your kindness, I offer you a gift."

"Goblins do not give gifts," Caelen says, his voice low and menacing. "They make bargains that benefit only themselves."

"Not all of us are wicked," Glenda says. Her gaze sweeps to me. "But he is right that we do make bargains. But what I offer will not harm you, I swear."

Caelen bristles. "Say nothing to her, Lyana. Gather your pack. We are leaving."

Glenda shakes her head and gestures toward the door. "Do you not see the storm still raging beyond these walls? Your human bride would catch her death out there. And that is something neither you nor I want."

"Why do you pretend to care?" Caelen snaps.

"You hesitate to kill me because something inside you recognizes that I mean you no harm," she replies. "It is fate that led you to me. I saw it in a vision many nights ago." A sly smile curls her lips. "Just as it was fate that bound you both together."

Her eyes slide to me again. "There are two paths before you, Princess Lyana and Prince Caelen. In one, you unite and rule over the kingdoms of Eryadon and Rivenyl, ensuring its peace." She pauses. "And in the other, the princess dies."

Caelen growls even louder. "You will die before you touch her," he grinds out.

"How?" The question escapes me almost at the same time as his threat.

Anger rolls off Caelen in heated waves as he stands protectively in front of me.

Glenda snaps her fingers, and a mirror appears in her hand. She meets Caelen's eyes impassively. "Calm yourself, Prince. Allow me to explain."

CHAPTER 36

CAELEN

N arrowing my eyes, I study the mirror. A subtle, green glow permeates the frame and handle. It is magic, but it does not feel sinister.

As if sensing my question, Glenda holds it out to us. Bright light flashes across the mirror a moment before it reveals Queen Rina and Fredrik, locked together in a lover's embrace.

My mouth falls open and Lyana gasps as Rina's image fades away to reveal a goblin woman with long, purple hair and pale lavender skin. Noticeably absent is her swollen abdomen.

"I... don't understand," Lyana whispers in shock. "Rina is—"

"A goblin and a blood witch," Glenda says, finishing her sentence. "Yes. And she is not with child either. That was a glamour meant to fool you and your father into trusting her, whilst manipulating Fredrik to believe it was his child as well."

"Can Fredrik see her true form?" Lyana asks.

Glenda shakes her head.

The image fades, replaced by our reflections. "Why do you show us this?" I ask, eyeing her warily.

Magic flows through my veins, arcing through my body and sparking across the tips of my fingers, ready to strike if this goblin dares try anything.

Glenda's gaze drops to my hands. "I promise that I mean you no harm, Prince Caelen. You or your mate." She darts a glance at Lyana. "Just as you have learned that not all humans are bad, surely you must realize that not all goblins are evil." She pauses. "Yes, we are few and far between, but we *do* still exist."

Despite her words, I am hesitant to trust her. I want to put as much distance between us and this goblin as possible. "We are leaving," I state firmly. "And if you wish to live, you will not try to stop us."

Glenda sighs heavily. "If you leave now, you will be unable to save her."

I go still.

"Please," she pleads. "Let me help you."

"Why would you offer to aid us?" I ask. "Why should we trust you?"

"Because if you do not, she will most assuredly die." She turns to Lyana. "Your mother made a bargain with me long ago."

"My mother? Why would she come to you?"

"She was desperate for a child. My magic gave her two. You and your brother. But there is always a price for such things, especially a spell as potent as this. I warned her, but she refused to listen. I have had to live with this guilt, and that is why I help you now."

Lyana studies her in disbelief.

Fear tightens my chest, followed quickly by anger as I

glare at the witch. "Tell me: what price did your magic exact for this bargain? And how can we break it?"

She swallows hard. "I cannot tell you how to break a spell I have cast as the result of a bargain. You understand magic; you know the rules of binding prevent me from speaking of it."

I growl low in my throat. "You *will* speak of it to me," I grind out as I step toward her, readying to cast.

With a flick of her wrist, she throws up a barrier spell, but I easily step through. Her eyes widen. "Wait!" She holds out the mirror. "I cannot speak of it, but the mirror can show you."

"Show me what?" I grit through my teeth.

"The future—that which will come to pass."

I level an icy glare at her. "How do I know what it will divulge is true?"

"Your magic is strong. Surely you can feel even now that this mirror does not lie."

She is right. Nothing about this mirror suggests malevolence, but something does seem slightly off. I take it from her, studying it warily.

"While the magic itself is not evil, this mirror can still do harm," she says. "Those who use it too often go mad."

"Why?" Lyana asks behind me.

As I stare down at the glass, I understand the witch's words. "Some things are best left alone," I murmur. "Knowledge of the future can be a powerful and dangerous thing."

Lyana's hand on my back draws my attention as she moves to my side. She glances at the mirror and then up at me. "Then, we will only use it once."

I nod in agreement.

The witch touches the frame and closes her eyes. "Mirror, mirror in my hand, show them the future that they must understand."

Images flare across the smooth surface, moving so fast many of them are blurred. A silver dragon flies overhead, raining down fire upon Fredrik's forces.

Suddenly, I'm transported; I am standing in the midst of battle. I look down and gasp as Lyana lies in my arms; her body limp and her eyes fixed upon mine with a glazed expression. I pull her to my chest, raging and crying out for help.

She disappears and a *sylven* apple is in my hand—a symbol of hope and life among my people. I lift my head, and find a glass coffin laid out upon a gray stone slab; Lyana inside it, her eyes closed in death.

Terror seizes my heart and the vision falls away, leaving me shaken.

"What dark sorcery is this?" I growl at the witch. "I will kill you where you stand."

CHAPTER 37

LYANA

As Caelen and I stare in the mirror, our reflections fade, replaced by a hazy fog. Images flash by so quickly, I can barely register them. A silver dragon releases a stream of fire over Eryadon's castle and Fredrik's guards.

I'm transported to a field of battle. The armies of men, elves, wolves, and dwarves rage around me. Axes and swords clash in great devastation and blood.

The images shift and blur. I fall back and Caelen cries out. He gathers me in his arms, brushing the hair back from my face as my vision goes black.

I blink and the world returns. My heart hammers in my chest as my panicked breath comes in short, clipped pants. The dark memory of my death fills my mind as I stare transfixed at the bare earthen floor. "I will die," I whisper to myself in shock.

Caelen flings the mirror across the room. It slams against the wall, exploding into shards of glass that rain down upon the floor. He growls and spins to the goblin. "What dark sorcery is this? I will kill you where you stand. You said it would show me how to save her."

My eyes snap up to find the witch's full of fear as Caelen looms over her, seething with anger. "I—I never said—"

He raises his hand before her, curling his fingers as if gripping something. My jaw drops as Glenda's body jerks up, her feet hovering over the earthen floor, kicking wildly as she grasps at her throat, held by the invisible force of Caelen's power.

Now, I understand why Father forbade Caelen's people to use magic in Eryadon. How they have not already conquered the known world with this power is beyond my understanding. Although she is a goblin, I cannot let him kill her. "Caelen, stop!"

He straightens, dropping his hand to his side as the witch also drops to the floor.

She clutches at her throat, coughing and spluttering. "The mirror shows you the future," she wheezes. "There must be a way to save her. Surely, you saw something that—"

"What was the price of your magic?" His eyes burn with anger. "Tell me the price of the bargain you made with the queen!"

"She would bear two children, but they would both die before they came to the throne."

He stills, rage rolling off his shoulders in heated waves. He curls his hands into fists at his sides and a blast of wind explodes through the cottage, flinging the door open and blasting out the windows as he roars his anger to the sky.

The witch cowers before him, trembling.

"Caelen, stop!"

"Do not go near her, Lyana, she—"

"She didn't have to tell us anything, Caelen, but she did," I snap. I turn to the witch. "My younger sister died with my mother during childbirth. Her and my brother did not live to ascend to the throne."

Glenda shakes her head. "Your younger sister was not conceived as a result of the bargain. You and your brother were the ones born of magic."

"Tell me what is in those images, in the mirror, that can save my mate," Caelen demands.

"Your mate's death is the price of a bargain forged by magic, but there is always an out to any bargain. You know this, High Elf Prince. Or has it been so long that your people have forgotten the ancient ways? Study the mirror. Decipher the clues. You were fated to each other for this reason, Prince Caelen. *You* are the one who can save her life."

Still enraged, Caelen lunges for the witch, but she disappears in the blink of an eye.

An angry roar rips from his throat before he rushes to the broken mirror and picks up the largest shard. "Mirror, mirror in my hand," he murmurs.

I stare transfixed as he peers at the mirror, his mouth open and eyes wide as he studies whatever it is showing him. When he pulls back, he runs a hand roughly through his hair. "You must be present at the battle," he mutters, more to himself than to me.

"What do you mean?"

"I asked the mirror to show me the future based on the choice to keep you from battle," he replies, not looking away. "But it is a decision that cannot be changed. You must be there."

Caelen speaks the enchanted words again and my jaw drops as I watch him staring into the mirror. This is what the witch meant about people going mad.

I move to his side, placing my hand on his forearm. "Caelen, stop."

"Just a few more," he mutters, still not looking away from whatever he is seeing.

"Caelen!" His head snaps up, his eyes refocusing as they meet mine. My mouth dries as I notice dark lines beneath his eyes that were not there a moment ago. I cup his face gently. "Stop, please."

His eyes search mine and he strokes my cheek. "You do not understand. I have to do this now. While I am strong. Each use drains my magic. And each time I can feel it take that much longer to recover."

I reach for the shard, but Caelen pulls it away from my grasp. "Give it to me," I demand.

When he hesitates, I sigh. "I'll put it in my bag. We can consult it later. But not now."

His brow furrows and I gesture to the outside. "The storm has passed. We have to keep moving. We have to get to Solwyck."

"Fine." He casts an icy glare throughout the cottage. "Let us leave this cursed place."

As soon as we step through the gate, he turns and raises his arms, slashing them through the air. Magic arcs from his fingers and races toward the already crumbling structure, razing it to the ground.

CHAPTER 38

LYANA

As we continue through the woods toward Solwyck, Caelen is silent. Every so often he squints at my pack, and I know he is desperate to use the mirror again. His gaze meets mine and the dark circles under his eyes tempt me to throw it far away into the woods where he cannot find it.

Knowing that it drains him, I would rather he not look at it ever again.

When we crest the hill and see the city of Solwyck laid out before us, I stare at it in awe. I heard of the destruction wrought by the dragon, but it is not as severe as I imagined. Although smoke stains the white stone buildings, we do not find the smoldering ash and ruin I expected. The people are busy rebuilding.

My gaze sweeps to the castle. The shimmering, pearlescent, white stone structure sits proudly atop the cliff wall overlooking the obsidian sands and the crystalline blue sea.

Its spiraling towers stretch proudly toward the pale blue sky overhead.

The last of the sun's rays reflect off the silver rooftops as the bold, blue and silver banner of Solwyck on the tallest tower waves in the wind.

From what I can tell, the castle appears to have survived the attack with very little damage, and I'm glad.

"Solwyck is not as much in ruin as I'd heard," Caelen murmurs, echoing my thoughts. "The people are already rebuilding."

"Yes, it's wonderful." I smile. "Let us hurry. The sun is already beginning to set, and I want to reach the castle before dark."

He nods, and we continue on the path.

"I remember visiting this place when I was a child." A wistful smile crests my lips. "My mother was cousin to the queen, Halla and Gerold's mother. I thought the city was a shining beacon next to the ocean; the castle reminded me of a sparkling pearl." I turn to Caelen. "Did you ever see it before now?"

"Only a few times. Our people are not friends."

"Of course," I murmur, more to myself than to him.

After all we've been through together, I forget that before our wedding, we were practically enemies. His kind do not normally like humans, nor do mine like his.

As if reading my thoughts, he turns to me. "You should walk ahead of me. I doubt High Elves are welcome here, and I do not want to draw any attention to you."

An idea occurs to me. "Here." I hold out the cloak Malak gave me. "You should wear this now."

He frowns.

I gesture to the city. "Solwyck's population is mostly human and the Merfolk who live along the harbor. You're right. You *will* stand out without this. Malak said it would conceal the wearer's appearance. Now put it on."

Reluctantly, he takes the garment from me, and I watch in wonder as it conceals his true form. He could pass as completely human. His glittering green eyes are now pale and dim, and his ears are missing their pointed tips. I blink at him. "Is this what it did for me? Completely change my appearance?"

He shrugs. "I do not know. I can see beyond this magic to your true form."

"Naturally." I purse my lips in mock irritation. "Yet another way we are inferior to your kind."

"That is not what I meant," he quickly adds.

My lips curve up in a faint smile. "I know. I was just teasing you."

His eyes search mine, something akin to hope flashing briefly behind them as his mouth quirks up slightly at the edges.

He follows me through the streets, where people study us warily. After the dragon attack, I suppose Solwyck does not get as many visitors as it used to. This city used to be a bustling hub of trade. Considering the impressive rebuilding efforts, I suspect it will not be very long before Solwyck is restored to the prosperous place it once was.

When we reach the castle near the edge of the water, I take Caelen's hand and pull him to a halt. "Let me do the talking, all right?"

He frowns. "What are you—"

I put a finger to his lips to silence him. "Trust me."

He nods and allows me to lead him to the palace gates.

The tall spires of the castle stretch toward the sky like giant, iridescent pillars holding up the clouds. The gates are perfectly polished blue metal, with depictions of the sea twisted into the gaps in a lovely display.

"Halt!" one guard calls. "What business do you have here?"

I stand tall and proud. "I am Princess Lyana of Eryadon, and I have come to visit my dear cousins, King Gerold and Princess Halla. Inform them that I have arrived."

The two guards blocking the gates share a shocked glance.

"Princess Lyana?" asks the first. He eyes Caelen, but when he sees nothing but a human beneath his cloak, his shoulders relax. "Where is the High Elf Prince who stole you? How did you escape that filth?"

Caelen bristles beside me but says nothing.

I clear my throat. "Will you announce my arrival or just stand here asking questions?"

A flush creeps across his face, and they scramble to open the gates. One guard leads us into the palace as I clutch Caelen's hand.

He leans toward me and whispers, "Is this wise?"

"Halla and Gerold are my cousins. Once we speak to them, I believe they will help us."

"I hope you are right," he murmurs.

I do too. It seems word has spread that Caelen stole me, when nothing could be further from the truth.

They lead us to a garden at the back of the castle overlooking the sea. Several vibrant, flowering bushes with large white and pink blooms line the pathway.

I recognize Halla immediately, seated on a bench, with her back to us. Her long red hair waves in the wind as she rests her head on the shoulder of a dark-haired man, who sits with his arm around her waist. They gaze out at the ocean. I squint at the sheen of his skin—or rather, his scales.

The scale pattern disappears beneath the fabric of his tunic and climbs up his neck, flesh-colored but easily visible. I blink several times when I notice the pointed tips of his ears, a bit sharper than Caelen's, and the short, black claws that cap his fingers.

Whatever he is, this man is not human.

"Princess Halla." The guard bows low before her. "Your cousin, Princess Lyana of Eryadon, is here to see you."

Wide-eyed, Halla and the man turn to me. Her face splits in a wide grin. She pushes herself off the bench and shakily stands. The strange man places a supporting hand beneath her elbow to help her. Her steps are slow and her legs appear weak as she walks toward me with great effort.

I heard Halla had been injured slaying the dragon that attacked their city. It left her paralyzed from the waist down. It is encouraging to see that she is able to walk again, even if her stride is not smooth. My mouth drifts open when I notice the slight swell of her abdomen.

She is with child.

I turn back to her companion. His glowing, blue eyes are unnatural—he is most definitely not human.

"Lyana? Is it really you?" She throws her arms around my neck. "I was so worried. We heard about the High Elves attacking the palace. Queen Rina sent word that they killed your father and Prince Caelen stole you away." She pulls back, tears in her eyes. "How did you escape?"

"Lyana?" a man's voice calls out and I recognize Gerold right away. With his short red hair and bright blue eyes, anyone would know he and Halla were siblings. He rushes toward me, embracing me warmly. "Thank goodness you are safe. We heard about what happened and feared the worst. We—"

The man next to Halla inhales sharply, then snarls as he pulls her behind him.

His glowing blue eyes burn with anger as he glares at Caelen. "What are you?" he growls. "Stop hiding behind magic and show your true face."

Caelen removes his hood, and the magic falls away, revealing his true form. "I am Prince Caelen of Rivenyl."

Halla and Gerold both gasp.

Two guards raise their weapons, but I quickly move to Caelen's side to shield him.

Gerold holds out a hand to his guards. "Wait!"

I take Caelen's hand firmly in mine. "He is my husband. It is not as you've heard. Please, allow me to explain."

Halla gestures to the strange man. "This is my husband, Prince Errik of the Mer."

"You are Mer?" Caelen asks, his gaze traveling over the man's shape and down to his very human-looking legs. "How is this possible?"

"It seems we both have much to discuss," Halla says.

As I explain Fredrik's attack and my stepmother's deception, Gerold, Halla and Errik stare at me in shock.

Gerold clears his throat. "You are certain Queen Rina is a goblin?"

Tears sting my eyes, but I blink them back. "I thought she truly loved us," I tell them, remembering the three of us together. "Father was so excited about the baby. I was too." My voice quavers.

Caelen takes my hand, squeezing it gently. Anger replaces my sadness as I think on her lies. "She tried to convince me to marry Fredrik. I'm sure it was their plan to kill both Father and me. But when Caelen arrived, they changed their plans... blaming the High Elves for Father's death and my disappearance."

Gerold gives me a pained smile. "I am sorry for all you have been through, Lyana. But know that you are safer here with us. We will protect you."

CHAPTER 39

CAELEN

While Lyana speaks with Halla, Gerold turns his attention back to me. "Was your journey here difficult?"

I nod. "They sent two Wolf shifter hunters after us. One was Prince Malak—Fredrik's brother. He found us and warned us of this."

Gerold sits forward in his seat. "Why would Prince Malak betray his own family?"

"He swore a blood oath to Lyana's brother—Arthur—for having saved his life. He expressed hatred toward his own brother and father as well for trying to kill someone he loved."

Gerold places a hand firmly on my shoulder. "Thank you for bringing Lyana safely to us. We will protect her from Fredrik and Rina. We will not forget what you have done for our cousin." He sits back. "I will see to it that you are provided a horse and carriage to travel the rest of the way to Rivenyl. Or a ship, if you'd prefer to travel by sea."

My heart falters as I process his words. I look at Lyana, observing as she smiles at Halla and Errik. I had not even considered that she might wish to stay here, with the only family she has left.

Gerold follows my line of sight. "You are probably wondering about Errik's legs, I assume."

It was not in the forefront of my thoughts, but I *am* curious. I tip my head to the side. "How is this possible?"

I listen as Gerold explains how Errik is able to shift from man to Mer in the water and back again. "And their child?" I ask, darting a glance at Halla's swollen abdomen.

"The Healers assure us their daughter will be like her father," Gerold explains. "Able to go back and forth between land and sea."

Gerold excuses himself to go speak with Lyana, leaving me alone with my thoughts.

I keep thinking of the fear in her eyes the other night when I almost marked her. She looked at me as if I were a monster. A dull ache settles in my chest as my gaze drifts to her.

I wonder if she will choose to stay here and annul our marriage. According to the traditions of her people, our union was never consummated and she would be well within her rights to do so.

I do not doubt that she will keep our original bargain for my people to help her regain her throne in exchange for a permanent and binding peace. I love her and I do not want to lose her. But I will not force her to remain with me if she does not want me anymore. Especially if she is afraid of me.

Errik appears at my side, pulling me back from my dark thoughts. He flashes a bright grin. "Tell me: is your human mate as frustrating as mine?"

When I frown, he adds with a smirk, "They are beautiful, yet so very stubborn, are they not?"

I arch a brow. "You speak truth," I offer, and he laughs.

My expression falls, however, as my gaze returns to her. "We spoke human vows of binding, but we are not true mates."

His brow furrows. "But you are married?"

"Yes. It is… complicated."

Errik nods. "So it seems." He pauses. "What will you do?"

He studies me a moment, waiting patiently for me to answer.

Perhaps it is because he is Otherworldly being, like myself, that I feel comfortable speaking openly with him. I swallow against the knot in my throat as I force my eyes away from Lyana. "I made a deal with her that I would help her retake her throne. In exchange, she promised a binding peace treaty between Eryadon and Rivenyl."

Errik frowns. "But your marriage secures this already. Are you saying that you would annul your vows?"

"I will not force her to remain bound to me if she does not desire me as her mate." Sharp pain stabs at my chest.

"Ah." A smirk twists his lips. "I thought your people were known for masking their emotions, but I understand what it is that you do not say, High Elf. You *are* in love with her, but you do not know if she feels the same."

I study him a moment, not sure I like that this Mer can read me so easily.

He claps me on the shoulder. "I believe your worries may be unfounded. You may not be as handsome as a Mer," —he grins— "but from the way Lyana spoke of you to Halla, it seems your personality more than makes up for it, Elf."

I arch a brow, and he laughs heartily. "I am only teasing you, Caelen. After all, if we are to be cousins through bonding, I would very much like to be your friend."

He leans in. "How do you plan to retake the castle?"

"I hoped we could board a ship for my kingdom and gather Rivenyl's army, and—"

"What if you had the help of a dragon?"

My head jerks back. The image of the silver dragon from the mirror flashes through my mind. "You know of one that would help us?"

He nods. "There is a dragon who lives in Eryadon. I believe he might help you."

Dragons are selfish and arrogant creatures. They care only for treasure: gold, silver, gems, and such. Humans are nothing to them. "Why would he help us?"

"Because he is mated to a human."

"I have heard of this dragon, though I can still hardly believe it."

"I can assure you, it is true." A grin curves Errik's mouth. "They are quite happily mated, I might add."

My mind races with possibilities and I lean forward. "Tell me about him."

CHAPTER 40

LYANA

Halla cuts her eyes to Caelen as he stands across the room speaking with Errik. "He does not have you bewitched, does he?"

I laugh, but then sober when I realize she is serious. "No, he *does not*. He saved me, Halla. He got me out of the castle when Fredrik's guards attacked."

She takes my hand. "You are welcome to remain with us. Indefinitely," she adds.

Tears fill my eyes, but I blink them back. "I appreciate the offer. Truly. But I cannot allow Rina's betrayal to go unpunished. I have to retake the throne. Caelen and I are going to Rivenyl to gather their army."

"Gerold and I will send what help we can," she says. "But I fear it will not be much. We are still rebuilding."

"Thank you, Halla. You have no idea how much it means to me."

I appreciate her offer of help, but I fear it still may not be enough. Eryadon's castle is one of the most fortified in all the kingdoms. It was built for defense. It will be difficult to retake.

Errik and Caelen join us. Caelen announces, "Errik has some news you may wish to hear."

"What is it?"

Errik steps forward. "Did you know the dragon of Eryadon and his human mate are expecting a child?"

I'm surprised. "No, I had not heard this."

"And do you know who a dragon hates more than Elves, and Fae, and all other creatures combined?"

"No."

Caelen grins. "Wolf shifters."

"You are fortunate." Errik smiles. "The dragon and his mate will arrive here tomorrow."

"Why are they coming?" I ask.

"Our Healer, Althea, has been monitoring his mate's pregnancy."

I turn to Halla. "And... the people of Solwyck are all right with a dragon coming here after one of them tried to destroy your city?"

"At first, it was terrifying, for the people and for me," she explains. "But I realize that, just like people, not all dragons are malevolent. Veron is... different from other dragons."

Caelen and I exchange a knowing look. We both saw a dragon when we gazed into the mirror. We have shared nothing of this with the others and I'm not sure I want to. After all, Glenda warned that those who study it too long can go mad.

Caelen's eyes move to my pack, where I've stored the enchanted shard. I'm sure he is eager to consult it again, but I wish that he would not.

His eyes meet mine again and a silent agreement passes

between us. We'll keep the information about the mirror to ourselves. At least, for now.

After dinner, Halla informs us that rooms have been prepared for us to rest. One of the staff leads us up the stairs and down a long hallway. She stops in front of a large door and gestures to Caelen. "These are your chambers, Prince Caelen."

She turns to me and motions down the corridor. "Yours are this way, Princess Lyana."

Caelen's eyes flick to me but then lower as the woman continues on. "Wait," I tell her.

She spins to face me. "I would prefer to stay in the same room as my husband."

Her brows pinch together and she blinks several times. "Of—of course, Princess." She bows low. "I… forgive me. I thought that—" She stops abruptly, her cheeks turning bright red. "I will inform the rest of the staff."

I give her a polite smile of dismissal. "Thank you. That will be all."

Caelen's eyes search mine as I take his hand. Together, we step into the room.

A king-size bed stands against the far wall, next to a fireplace, and a table and chairs sit in one corner. There is a large balcony with a beautiful view of the ocean and the shoreline below.

I am immediately drawn to the door that leads to the cleansing room with a huge sunken tub in the center. Already full of water, a fine mist of steam rises from the surface in invitation.

Caelen watches me silently, but it is easy to read the concern on his face. We still have not spoken of what happened between us. He probably still believes I'm afraid of him.

I hate that things are strained between us. I love him. Now, I must convince him that, despite my reaction, I am not afraid of him.

CHAPTER 41

LYANA

We each take turns in the cleansing room, bathing and dressing for bed. The soft, silken blue sleeping gown I find in the cleansing room is held up by two thin straps over my shoulders and only reaches mid-thigh. I drape the matching long robe to cover myself, tying the sash at my waist before I walk back into the bedroom.

It's quiet between us, and every time I glance over at Caelen I cannot help but notice the tense set of his shoulders. Dressed only in soft knit pants, the shadows and moonlight spilling into the room sculpt the thick planes of muscle that cover his body.

He moves with a grace that belies his lethal form as he steps out onto the balcony and stares at the sea.

A crisp, saline breeze blows gently from the ocean, tousling his short, blond hair as he leans forward on the railing. His hands grip the edge and he scans the water as if searching for something. Silver moonlight casts sparkling reflections across the rolling waves. I move up beside him and rest my hand over his.

He shifts his gaze to me, sadness easily read in his expression. "You do not have to stay with me, Lyana, if you do not wish."

I'm not sure if he's referring to this room or our marriage, but either way, my answer is the same. "I want to stay with you, Caelen."

"You owe me nothing, Lyana," he murmurs. "I will still help you, no matter what you decide about us. According to your traditions, our marriage can still be annulled and—"

I press a finger to his lips. I stare deep into his beautiful green eyes as I untie my robe and allow it to fall away, pooling at my feet. "Not after tonight," I whisper. I stretch up on my toes and wrap my arms around his neck.

His strong arms encircle my waist, drawing me close as his gaze holds mine. "You are not afraid of me?"

"Not of you." I cup his cheek. "Ever. I love you, Caelen. And I choose you as my husband and mate."

He touches my face, staring at me as if I were a rare and precious thing. "I choose you, Lyana," he whispers. "You are my mate, and I am yours."

Ever so gently, he leans in. He presses his lips to mine in a tender kiss and I open for him, curling my tongue around his and deepening our kiss.

Soft and gentle at first, it turns into something deep and sensuous, his desire matching mine. He lifts me in his arms and carries me to the bed.

He pulls back the covers and lays me reverently atop the sheets before moving over me. His eyes search mine a moment before I cup the back of his neck and pull his lips down to my own.

Caelen kisses me long and deep. He tastes of warm cinnamon. A soft moan escapes me as his hand glides across my skin to gently circle one breast.

I gasp as his thumb brushes over the already sensitive peak through the silken fabric of my gown.

I arch into him, wanting more. "Caelen," I breathe against his lips.

He growls in arousal and rips his mouth from mine, trailing kisses down my neck to my chest.

I run my fingers through his golden hair and trace the outlines of his pointed ears. He growls low in arousal as he dips his hand beneath the neckline of my gown, freeing my breast. He closes his mouth over the hardened tip and begins a gentle suction that sends pleasure rippling through me.

He turns his attention to my other breast, giving it the same intimate treatment as the first before he pulls back. His green eyes hold mine, full of desire and hunger, as he stares down at me, his fangs fully extended.

I reach up and caress his cheek, making sure my gaze remains locked on his. "I'm not afraid," I whisper softly.

"You are certain you want me?" he asks, his voice thick with longing.

"Yes."

He lifts his left hand and I watch as his claws extend and he slices a line down the fabric of my dress, baring me to his gaze.

"*Ashalan, Ashalik, Kaltoryn,*" he whispers words in the Elvish tongue, and although I do not know what they are, I understand their meaning in the way they escape his lips in awe-filled reverence.

He pulls back and carefully takes my heel in his hand and presses a tender kiss to the inside arch of my foot. His gaze holds mine as he traces his lips and his tongue up my calf to my inner thigh.

"Open for me," he whispers against my skin. "I want to taste you on my tongue."

My heart pounds in anticipation as I part my thighs. His eyes snap up to mine, full of possession. "You are mine," he growls.

His gaze holds my own as he guides my legs over his shoulders. He dips his head and drags his tongue through my already slick folds.

I gasp as he reaches the sensitive bundle of nerves at the apex. A low growl rumbles his chest; the vibration moves straight through me, igniting fire deep in my core.

I dig my heels into his shoulders as he continues to tease my sensitive flesh with his tongue, leaving me breathless and panting beneath him.

He bands an arm across my hips to anchor me as I writhe under his attentions. "Caelen," I barely manage to breathe through my pleasure. "It's too much. I'm going to—"

My entire body goes taut like a bowstring and then I'm coming. I cry out his name as wave after wave of pleasure washes over and through me.

I've not even recovered from my orgasm when he moves back up my body, sealing his mouth over mine and stealing the breath from my lungs in a searing kiss.

His length is hard against my inner thigh, but we're separated by the thin barrier of his clothing. I run my hands down his body, tracing my fingers over every delicious dip and curve of his heavily muscled form and sliding them beneath the waistband of his pants.

Gently, I push them down his hips, freeing his erection.

He pulls back and my gaze moves down his body to study him. He's much larger than I thought he would be. And although I've had no experience, I've seen images of men and know he is very different from a human male.

Cautiously, I reach for him. He's so thick, my fingers do

not entirely reach around him. His length is covered in ridges and his tip is flared wide at the end. "My *stav* is different than you expected," he whispers, but I note the hint of worry that laces his tone.

"I've never done this before," I admit. "You seem so... large compared to the images I've seen of human men."

He cups my chin. "We do not have to—"

I silence him with a kiss. "I want to make love to you, Caelen. I want to be yours."

He drops low and rolls onto his back, pulling me on top so that my legs straddle his hips. His gaze holds mine as he trails his fingers over my body in a gentle caress. "You are so beautiful," he whispers.

I lean down and kiss him. His stav is hard beneath me. When I pull back I notice the bead of liquid that gathers on the end. Carefully, I raise up on my knees and wrap my hand around his length.

His eyes stare deep into mine and the breath stutters from my lungs as I slowly lower myself onto him. A low groan escapes his lips as I take him inside me.

Tight heat blooms in my core as he pushes through my barrier, sinking all the way to the hilt deep within. We gaze at each other in mutual wonder of our bodies joined as one. I've never felt so full.

Slowly, I begin to move, inhaling sharply at the delicious friction of his ridges as they move against my inner walls. He wraps his hands around my hips. "So tight," he rasps.

He sits up and I wrap my legs around his back as he gathers me to his chest. His heart pounds against mine as we move as one. His tongue strokes against my own and I'm lost in sensation.

His hands are everywhere as he claims me with each gentle thrust of his hips up into mine. He whispers words of love and devotion against my lips. Nothing exists outside of this moment and the joining of our bodies as we move as one.

Pleasure coils tight in my core. I'm so close to the edge, but I don't want this to end. "Caelen," I breathe into his mouth. "I'm almost—"

Passion burns in my vein as desire builds deep within. Each thrust of his hips up into mine becomes stronger and deeper as we chase our release. His masculine scent surrounds me and I'm lost in the feel of our bodies joined as one.

The base of his stav expands in my channel, almost to the point of pain, but not quite. I feel a slight pinch deep inside, but it's quickly replaced with intense pleasure that makes me gasp. "What is—"

"My knot," he rasps. "And the tip of my stav sealing over the entrance to your womb."

The sensation of his body locked with mine is too much. My head falls back and my lips part on a moan as his length begins to pulse in my channel.

He growls and then sinks his fangs into my neck, marking me as his. The pain quickly disappears and I fall over the edge, crying out his name in ecstasy as he erupts deep inside me, filling me with the delicious warmth of his seed.

It feels as though it goes on forever, triggering another orgasm; this one even stronger than the last.

I'm not even recovered when he twists and flips me onto my back. His stav is still knotted inside me. He stares down at me, his gaze full of possession. A low moan escapes me as he begins to stroke long and deep.

"You are mine," he growls.

I'd heard that human men need time to recover after their release, but it seems it is not this way with High Elves.

Caelen seals his mouth over mine in a claiming kiss. "*Ashal'veh*, Lyana," he breathes against my lips.

I cling to him, enjoying the feel of his powerful body moving over me. We make love several more times until I'm completely spent and unable to keep my eyes open any longer.

He skims the tip of his nose alongside mine and then presses a tender kiss to my lips. "Sleep, my Lyana," he whispers softly in my ear.

Closing my eyes, I allow myself to drift away in his arms.

CHAPTER 42

LYANA

When I wake, the first rays of the sun are just barely visible, bathing the room in a soft, orange glow. I stretch. The muscles ache between my thighs, but in a good way, reminding that I've been thoroughly claimed by my High Elf husband.

Caelen is on the balcony, and I observe as he holds the mirror shard in his palm. His brows furrow deeply in contemplation as he murmurs the words of enchantment, staring into the future as he tries to find a way around what the magic has foretold.

He clenches his jaw, and tries again. The witch's warning rings in my head. Those who stare too long can go mad.

I pull my robe over my shoulders and walk up behind him, resting my hand lightly on his arm to draw his attention to me. His expression is pained as his gaze meets mine. He swallows hard. "I can see no course that does not result in—"

I press a finger to his lips to silence him.

He takes my hand and brushes a tender kiss across my

knuckles as he continues despite my protest. "I keep seeing the dragon, a *sylven* apple, and you in a glass—" his voice breaks on the last word and he turns away from me. He swallows hard and stares out at the sea a moment before he swings back and crushes me to his chest.

He runs a hand through my hair. Gripping the long strands between his fingers, he tips my head back to face him. Caelen cups my cheek and drops his forehead gently to mine, his eyes bright with tears.

My heart clenches. "How long have you been doing this? Staring into the mirror?"

"Hours," he admits.

"Give it to me," I tell him.

He shakes his head. "I must keep trying. The answer is there. It has to be. It—"

"Give me the mirror," I state firmly. "Now."

Reluctantly, he hands it over. Before he can stop me, I fling the shard out into the sea.

"How could you do that? That was our only chance to figure this out."

I cup his cheek. "The witch said that those who stare too long into the mirror can go mad. I'll not have that happen to you, my love."

"But I could have found a way to save you, Lyana. Even if I take you to Rivenyl and we never return to Eryadon, you still—"

"We'll find a way, Caelen."

Anger flashes behind his eyes, but he says nothing. Clenching his jaw, he retrains his face into a perfect, stoic mask; one I haven't seen since the day we first met… when we were nothing more than strangers.

He turns and heads back into the room. He changes quickly and then begins placing our belongings into our packs. It is easy to see he is upset, but I don't want things to be this way between us. "Caelen, I—"

"We're going somewhere far from here," he says. "I am taking you to Anara. The Fae Prince Ryvan has taken a human mate. We are allies with them. They will not turn us away if we wish to remain in their kingdom, behind the Veiled wall that keeps all others out."

"I'm not going to Anara, Caelen. I am going to ask the dragon to help me, and I'm going to take back Eryadon, with or without your help."

"Why?" he asks, frustration easily read in his features. "Why not go somewhere else? Live out our lives in peace?"

"Because my people have been left under the rule of those who murdered their rightful king," I state firmly. "It does not matter where we go or what we do, Rina will search for me, Caelen. I'm the rightful heir to the throne. Their position is not secure so long as I am alive." I take both his hands in mine. "Don't you understand? I cannot run from this. No matter how much I wish that I could."

"What about us?" he asks, mouth pinched with tension. "Do you not care what it would do to me if I lost you?"

"Of course I care, Caelen."

"Then, I am begging you to listen to me," he pleads. "Please, Lyana."

"I have to do this, Caelen. I cannot just abandon my people."

His nostrils flare, and he turns back to his pack, filling it with our supplies.

"What are you doing?" I ask, my voice tight.

"I am going to Rivenyl."

My heart stops and my stomach twists in a violent knot. Tears gather in the corner of my eyes, but I blink them back. "If... that is what you want."

"It is," he says, not bothering to look up at me. "Come with me."

"Please, Caelen, do not ask me to abandon my people."

"Fine. I will not."

With that, he stands and starts for the door. He grips the handle and then pauses. "Goodbye, Lyana."

He turns the knob and steps out into the hallway. Traitorous tears escape my lashes and roll down my cheek. I open my mouth to say something, but the words will not come. I'm frozen in place as devastation fills me.

He drops his bag and turns toward me. He crosses the room in less than five steps and gathers me in his arms. "Why did the gods curse me with such a stubborn mate?" he groans as he holds me close. "Are you really so determined to do this?"

"Were you really going to leave?" I ask, my heart in my throat.

Sighing heavily, he shakes his head. He brushes the tears from my cheek and I notice the ones of his own that he struggles to hold back. "No. I was bluffing. Praying you would follow... beg me not to leave and then agree to run away to Anara with me."

Relief fills me along with a healthy dose of anger. I glare up at him despite my tears. "That was a terrible plan. What kind of husband plays with his wife's emotions that way?"

He places a finger under my chin, tipping my face up to his. "The kind who would rather she be safe and angry at him, than watch her rush headlong into danger. I would not care if you hated me forever, as long as it meant you were safe." He pulls me to his chest, running his fingers through my long, dark hair.

And gods help me, I melt into his embrace.

I tip my head back to look up at him. "The words you

spoke to me last night, in your Elvish tongue, what do they mean?"

He presses a tender kiss to my forehead. "I love you more than anything, Lyana." He murmurs, pressing another to my cheek. "My heart is no longer my own." His lips brush mine, and he whispers against them. "It is yours, my beautiful, human wife."

I cup his cheek. "What are the words for *I love you* in your language?

"*Ashal'veh*," he breathes. Closing his eyes, he leans into my touch. He turns and presses another kiss to my palm. "Ashal'veh, my Lyana."

I brush my lips to his and whisper against them. "Ashal'veh, my Caelen."

CHAPTER 43

CAELEN

We gather with Gerold, Halla, Errik, and Healer Althea in the gardens, awaiting the dragon's arrival. A crisp, saline breeze drifts up from the ocean below, mixing with the lovely fragrance of all the blooming flowers around us. We sit on one of the many stone benches that surround a fire pit as the dull roar of the waves fills the air.

Halla, Gerold and Lyana share stories of the time they spent together here as children. It seems they were very close when they were young, and it warms my heart to see how wonderful they are to my mate, despite not having seen her in many years.

I study Healer Althea. She sits tall and proud, her shoulders back and her silver hair woven tightly to her head in a series of intricate braids as she recounts the hair-raising story of how she once caught them all jumping into the ocean from Halla's balcony when they were children.

Errik informs me that Althea is half Mer, like he and

Halla's daughter will be. This is why the dragon trusts her to assess his mate—because she is not completely human.

My gaze drops to Halla's slightly swollen abdomen and irrational envy fills me as Errik holds her close, resting his palm over her belly as he presses a tender kiss to her temple.

I want a future with Lyana, filled with children and laughter. My thoughts return to the images from the mirror. I have to find a way to save her. Even if the cost is my life.

A bellowing roar splits the air, freezing my blood. I whip my head toward the sound and stand as I see the silver dragon flying toward us. He is just as I've seen in the mirror.

Despite knowing he is not here to attack, panic snakes down my spine. I make sure Lyana is behind me as he circles overhead.

My eyes widen. I've never seen a dragon up close. He is much larger than I'd imagined. His silver scales shimmer with an iridescent glow beneath the sun's rays; his massive wings stirring up dirt and debris as he hovers overhead. The wind whips wildly around us and I gather Lyana close to shield her.

As soon as he touches down, he shifts instantly into his two-legged form, catching his mate around the waist and carefully lowering her feet to the ground.

Silver scales cover his entire body. He has two small, black horns just above his temples, at the edge of his short-cropped, black hair. His fingers and toes are tipped with lethal, black claws and his emerald green, reptilian eyes study us warily as he tugs his mate close to his side.

She appears so fragile next to him. The top of her head barely reaches his chin. Her blonde hair cascades down in a long braid that hangs over one shoulder and her deep blue eyes practically sparkle as they meet Halla's.

My gaze drops to her abdomen, heavy with their child. The dragon steps protectively in front of his mate and levels an icy glare at me, baring his sharp fangs. "What business do you have here, High Elf?"

Instinctively, I pull Lyana behind me again and bare my fangs in return.

Dragons have long been enemies of Elves.

Errik steps between us, holding up his hands. "Stop," he says. "Veron, this is—"

"A High Elf," Veron cuts him off. Narrowing his eyes, he flicks his tail behind him in agitation as he issues a threatening growl. "Why is he here?"

His mate steps in front of him and smacks at his chest. "Veron, stop it," she states firmly. "You do not have to growl at every new person we meet. This is why we don't have many friends."

I suck in a quick breath and brace myself, worried he will unleash his wrath upon this small, delicate human.

Instead, his expression softens as he turns his attention to her. "I am only trying to keep you and our fledgling safe, my beautiful mate."

My beautiful mate? I blink several times as I study them, shocked.

She takes his hand. "I know, my love. But not everyone means us harm."

She turns to me and Lyana. "I am Alara, and this is Veron." She glances at him. "He really is a wonderful man. He just needs some time to warm up to you. That's all."

He thrusts out his chest. "I *am not* a man. I am a dragon."

She sighs and purses her lips. "Everyone knows this, my love. I was just making conversation."

He circles her waist with his arm, curling a wing protectively around her side as he studies me. "Who are you?"

I take Lyana's hand. "I am Prince Caelen of Rivenyl. This is my mate, Princess Lyana of Eryadon."

Alara gasps, clamping her hand over her mouth, her eyes

wide. "Queen Rina said you killed the king and stole the princess."

Veron snarls, baring his deadly fangs.

Lyana raises her hands in a placating gesture. "That is not what happened. My stepmother lied. She and Prince Fredrik are responsible for my father's death. Caelen saved me. He has been protecting me ever since."

"Queen Rina is a goblin," I add, remembering that Errik confided in me how much Veron hates their kind.

"Vile creatures," Veron grumbles. "Goblins *and* Wolf shifters."

Lyana steps forward. "I am here before you today to seek your aid, Veron." She straightens her shoulders as he studies her warily, tipping up her chin. "You are a citizen of Eryadon, and I ask that you help your rightful queen retake her throne."

His brows draw together, obviously shocked by her words.

Here is the moment I'd feared. The one where he realizes it would make more sense for *him* to take the throne or simply burn and lay waste to the kingdom, gathering its riches to add to his treasure hoard. There is no reason for him to help.

His gaze locks onto hers. "Not long ago your father tried to have me killed."

"But he did not," she counters. "Not after he found out about your human mate."

His emerald eyes shift to me. "And what about the High Elves? You have married their prince. Do you intend to make him your king?"

Dragons and Elves have been enemies for hundreds of years, and I doubt he will help no matter her answer.

"Whether my husband is crowned king or consort is *my* decision." She stands regally before him, pulling the mantle of rule over her like a heavy cloak. The same way she appeared before me the first time we met. "Our marriage was formed to ensure peace between our two warring kingdoms. To stand united against those who would see us fall, like the Orcs. If the High Elves can make peace with humans, I do not see why such an agreement cannot be brokered between Dragons and Elves."

He opens his mouth as if to protest, but she continues.

"You may be a powerful and deadly dragon, but what will you do if Fredrik and Rina send their armies to your castle?"

He bristles. "I burned every knight that your father sent to end me. None of them could stand against a dragon."

"This is true. But you were alone then. Now you are mated and expecting a child. When one loves, it is an unimaginable joy… but, it does not come without its own perils. Our hearts no longer belong to us." She takes my hand, squeezing it gently as she repeats my words from this morning. "They belong to our beloved, and this makes us vulnerable to enemies who would use that love against us."

Veron curls his tail protectively around Alara's ankle as he pulls her even closer. "You speak truth." He tips his head to the side, studying her a moment before he adds. "I will help you retake your kingdom, Queen Lyana." He turns to me, his nostrils flaring. "But first, I must have the word of your mate, that he and his people will not be a threat to me or my family."

I meet his eyes evenly. "You have my most solemn vow."

We bid farewell to Halla, Errik, and Gerold. Halla hugs Lyana one more time, tears in her eyes. "Please, be careful, Lyana. And when this is all over, come visit us again. I have missed spending time with you, my dear cousin."

"I will," my mate replies.

Gerold turns to us both. "I will send as many men as I can. Send word once you are ready and we will be there."

Lyana hugs him tight. "Thank you, Gerold."

"You are family, Lyana. We will always be there for you." He looks to me and arches a brow. "And now that you are family as well, I'll expect better trade negotiations with your people."

"Done," I tell him.

I glance over his shoulder, observing as the dragon says goodbye to his mate.

There is always an out to any bargain. The witch's words repeat in my mind, and for the first time since I gazed in that blasted mirror, hope sparks in my chest.

CHAPTER 44

LYANA

Veron curls his arms and wings around Alara, holding her close. Tenderly, he rests his open palm against her swollen abdomen. "I will return as soon as I can, my *T'kara*."

A smile curls my lips. Halla told me that T'kara is the word for *treasure* in his language.

"I wish I could go with you, my dragon." A tear escapes her lashes as she cups his cheek.

"I will miss you every single moment I am away," he replies. He kneels and presses a tender kiss to her abdomen. "Both of you."

Caelen slips his arms around me from behind and I melt against him. His breath is warm in my ear as he whispers. "It seems I am not the only Otherworldly being that has fallen under the enchantment of a human."

A soft laugh escapes me. "Is that what you believe? That I've bewitched you somehow?" I tease.

He arches a brow. "If you have, it is a spell I willingly succumbed to."

Playfully, I hit at his chest. He growls low under his breath, spinning me to face him and gathering me close as he captures my lips in a searing kiss, stealing the air from my lungs.

When he pulls back, I study him curiously. "Your mood is light. What has changed, my love?"

"I believe I know what the mirror was trying to show me," he says. "The way out of the bargain that your mother made with the goblin."

I frown. "What is it?"

"The *sylven* apple," he explains. "I saw it in every version of the future the mirror showed me. It is a symbol of hope and life among my people. I always see it, along with the dragon. If we have one, we have the other, do we not? I believe it is the mirror's way of showing me that you will live."

A smile curves my mouth.

As we climb onto the dragon's back, worry steals my breath. We haven't even taken off yet, and I'm already afraid to look down. Caelen wraps an arm around my waist, pulling me back against the solid warmth of his chest. I twist my head back to face him. "Did I tell you I have a fear of heights?"

Tenderly, he combs the hair back from my face and brushes his lips against mine. "I will not let you fall, my Lyana."

Veron turns his massive head toward us, as he addresses Caelen. "You are certain your people will not try to attack me?"

"Not if you ensure they can see me on your back," Caelen replies.

He nods. "Done."

Veron extends his massive wings out to the sides, catching the wind beneath the great sails and lifting into the air.

I look down, watching as the world falls away beneath us with dizzying speed. My stomach roils and I groan. Closing my eyes, I lean back against Caelen.

"Do not look down," he whispers.

"Too late," I reply, swallowing against the bile rising in my throat.

"The view is stunning from up here," he says, his tone tinged with awe.

I open my eyes and stare out at the open sea and the cliff wall beside it. My fear and discomfort fall away as I gaze at the earth below us.

The sunlight casts sparkling, golden reflections across the ocean. Rolling waves crash against the shoreline. Several Mer swim beneath the clear, blue water, breaking through the surface and twisting in the air before diving back under. "It's incredible."

Veron dips his left wing to turn inland, heading toward what appears to be a solid mountain wall in the distance. I squint my eyes, studying it. It appears to be moving.

"What is that?" I ask Caelen.

"The Mists of Rivenyl," he replies. "Magic disguised as fog to deter enemies from crossing our borders."

"My brother spoke of this," I murmur as the memory returns. "Arthur nearly got lost in it once. It was your brother, Dhurvaen, who saved him."

Caelen chuckles softly in my ear. "Yes. Dhurvaen had captured him and was taking him back to our people to be imprisoned. Along the way, a Wraith attacked. Dhurvaen was injured and would have been slaughtered, but Arthur saved him."

"And set in motion the treaty of nonaggression between our people," I add.

Caelen nods, leaning against me. "Yes. I remember how tall and proud Arthur stood before my father when he demanded an end to the fighting between us."

"You met my brother?"

"Yes. He was very brave."

"I am glad he met you, my love."

"So am I," Caelen whispers.

Tears sting my eyes at the memory of Arthur, but I push down my sadness. I will have time to grieve later. Right now, I must focus on retaking my throne. It's what my brother would have done, if he were the one still here instead of me.

As we cross through the fog, I study the ground below in wonder. A dense forest canopy of trees with gorgeous purple, heart-shaped leaves stretch as far as the eye can see. Several of them have long, thick vines that hang down, covered in bioluminescent white blossoms.

As the sun dips low on the horizon, glowing white and yellow lights flit between the boughs as pixies flutter and twirl, lending the entire forest an ethereal, otherworldly glow.

The castle stands proudly up ahead, carved into the side of a mountain. Tall, circular, white towers stretch toward the clouds, their golden rooftops reflecting the last of the sun's rays like gleaming beacons.

Waterfalls cascade from the mountain above, spilling into collecting pools on each level of the palace before running through the gardens and into the city below. Each house and building is carved from the same white, pearlescent stone.

Cobblestones line the city walkways and paths. As night falls, several fairy lights begin to glow throughout the streets, the floating orbs appear as something straight out of a dream.

Everything is so beautiful; I don't know where to look.

As we draw closer, panicked shouts fill the air. The Elves scatter as Veron flies toward them, but he dips his wing to one side so they can see their prince flying on his back.

Several stop and stare, dumbfounded for a moment, before Caelen waves.

Cheers rise through the crowd along with several shouts. "Prince Caelen has returned!"

Veron lands in the courtyard outside the castle entrance with an audible *thump*.

Caelen slides off Veron's back and then reaches for me. He wraps his hands solidly around my waist and carefully sets me on the ground.

Several guards rush toward us, weapons at the ready. Caelen raises his hands. "Stand down," he commands. "The dragon is an ally, not an enemy."

They lower their weapons, staring in shock as Veron shifts into his two-legged form and walks up beside us. His green reptilian eyes narrow as he studies them warily.

"Where is my father?" Caelen asks the guards.

"The throne room, my Prince."

As we start for the doors, two figures rush out of the castle, and I realize they must be Caelen's father and sister.

His father is dressed in long, flowing green robes and a golden crown. He looks so much like Caelen, if not for the fine lines on his face, I'd mistake them as brothers.

Walking beside him must be Caelen's sister—Nurala. Her golden hair is twisted in an elegant braid that hangs down her back.

They both halt abruptly as soon as they notice Veron behind us.

"Guards!" Caelen's father cries out and the guards around

us instantly snap to attention again, brandishing their weapons.

A deep growl rips from Veron's throat as he flares his wings. Muscles ripple beneath his silver scales, as he readies to shift forms.

"Stop!" Caelen demands.

To his credit, the High Elf king's face reveals nothing of his shock. I only notice it in his eyes because I've spent so much time with his son that I can recognize their inability to hide emotion in their gaze.

Caelen's father studies Veron warily before turning to his son. "You brought a dragon to Rivenyl? What were you thinking?"

"He is not like other dragons," I interject, and Veron huffs.

"He has a human mate that is expecting their first child," Caelen adds.

King Kyvern's jaw drops, but he quickly snaps it shut. His brow furrows deeply. "A dragon mated to a human?" he asks incredulously.

Veron's nostrils flare.

"He brought us here," I explain. "He wants to make peace with your people."

"Peace?" King Kyvern asks. "Since when do dragons ever seek such a thing? They care only for blood, treasures, and gold."

"As if the Elves are any better," Veron snarls, baring his fangs.

Caelen steps between them. "We have much to discuss."

The king levels an icy glare at Veron. "He is not to step inside this castle. He will be bound and—"

"Try to bind me and I will burn your kingdom to ash," Veron growls.

"Veron," I call out, drawing his attention to me.

He turns to me, his gaze hard. "Come with me, Queen Lyana. We are wasting our time here."

Caelen's family and the guards snap their eyes to me. "You have a dragon at your command?" the king asks. This time the shock is easy to read in his features.

"Veron is my ally, not my subject," I correct.

Their expressions shift from fear and uncertainty to one of intense fascination as the king and the guards study Veron.

The High Elves are known for their stoicism. So, I'm surprised when Nurala rushes forward and throws her arms around Caelen. "First, we heard you were dead," she sobs. "But then rumors began that you had kidnapped the princess." She pulls back and her green eyes swim with tears. "I was so afraid we had lost you."

"All lies," he tells her as he returns her embrace. "I am here now. All is well."

He takes my hand, drawing me to his side. "Lyana, this is my sister, Nurala and my father, King Kyvern." He wraps a possessive arm around my waist. "And this is Lyana—my bride and my mate."

Their eyes snap to the claiming mark on my neck that Caelen gave me, and my cheeks heat under the intense scrutiny of their gazes.

His father's expression is an impassive mask as he looks to his son, but his eyes are bright with tears. He places a hand on Caelen's shoulder. It takes him a moment to speak. "When we received news of what happened, I feared the worst. I am glad you have returned to us, my son."

"I am glad to be home as well, Father."

Behind the king, I notice a familiar face at the same time as Caelen. He calls out. "Ruvaen? I thought you were dead," Caelen says. "How did—"

"I managed to escape the castle. I was wounded, but one

of the villagers took pity on me. They treated my injuries, and gave me a horse to make my way here."

Ruvaen steps forward and embraces Caelen warmly. "My boy, I am so glad to see you again." He turns to me. "And you as well, Princess. I am sorry about your father."

"Thank you." Tears threaten to fall, but I push them back down. "I am glad to see that you are alive. You are very important to Caelen."

His eyes dart to the mark on my neck and he flashes a warm smile. "It seems you are as well, Princess."

"She is queen now," Caelen interrupts. "The rightful heir to the throne of Eryadon, and we must gather our forces to help her retake it." Caelen looks to his father. "Let us go inside. There is much to discuss."

His father casts another wary look at Veron. "The dragon will remain here."

"No," I protest. "He will not. He is not your enemy, King Kyvern."

Caelen's father hesitates a moment before inclining his head. "Fine."

CHAPTER 45

LYANA

Caelen, Veron and I sit across from King Kyvern, Nurala, and Ruvaen, in the dining hall. Silver moonlight spills in through the large floor to ceiling windows that look out on the palace gardens and the river below.

The dining table is so long it appears as though it were meant for over a dozen people instead of just a few. Crystal plates and goblets and golden silverware are placed before us. A roaring fire near the head of the table heats the entire space.

Several glowing blue and green orbs are suspended throughout the room for lighting. Dozens of tapestries hang along the walls, depicting Elves in battle armor, facing down foes. I grimace when I notice the one showing a High Elf slaying a dragon.

Veron's eyes lock onto the tapestry with an angry glare. I notice he forgoes the silverware and uses his lethal claws to spear his food.

Large platters of food are arranged down the center of the long table, but I'm too nervous to eat. So much has happened and so much depends upon this meeting.

Veron will definitely tip the balance in the battle to regain my throne, but I worry he will not be enough now that I know Rina is a goblin witch. I need the help of Rivenyl's armies as well.

"I do not understand." Caelen's father looks to me. "What happened exactly? We were worried that you died." He turns to Ruvaen. "Ruvaen said he saw you take an arrow meant for my son when you were escaping."

"On the night of our wedding, Fredrik's men stormed the castle with the help of my stepmother—the queen. They murdered my father," I tell him, somehow managing to keep my voice even. "Fredrik would have killed me if not for your son. They intended to blame the death of myself and my father on Caelen and all those with him."

Caelen rests his hand over mine on the table. "Ruvaen's words are true," he adds. "When we were escaping, Lyana took an arrow meant for my back. She nearly died because of it."

His sister's eyes shine with tears. "You saved my brother."

"How can we ever repay you?" King Kyvern asks.

I regard him steadily. "I have come to ask for Rivenyl's aid in retaking my throne."

Kyvern sits back in his chair. "I have no desire to conquer Eryadon. I never have. I simply wanted to keep Rivenyl's borders intact. You are bound to my son. Rivenyl can be your home and no more High Elf blood need be spilled for you to remain here."

"And what if Fredrik and Rina do not stop with Eryadon?" I ask. "What if they decide to invade Rivenyl?"

"Then, we will defend our borders, as we always have."

His gaze darts to Veron. "You brought a dragon to my home. Was it to force my hand?"

Caelen growls beside me. He opens his mouth, but I begin.

"No," I state firmly. "My brother, Prince Arthur, came before you once and set in motion a treaty between our two kingdoms. Your son and I married to enforce it. I come before you now, as the rightful queen of Eryadon, asking that you honor it."

He studies me a moment before inclining his head. "Rivenyl will honor the alliance with Eryadon."

I dip my chin in a subtle nod of acknowledgment.

Kyvern turns to Veron. "Your kind are not known for your altruism, Dragon. Why would you do this?"

Veron tips up his chin, staring down at the king imperiously. "My mate is human and is carrying our fledgling. I will not have my son raised in a kingdom under the rule of a Goblin queen and a Wolf shifter king. The only two creatures I despise more than Elves and Fae."

Kyvern huffs. "And yet you want peace between us?"

Veron leans forward. "I will do anything to guarantee the safety of my mate and child."

Kyvern studies him as if he cannot believe it. "You have truly bound yourself to a human?"

"She is my *T'kara*," Veron grinds out. "My greatest treasure."

"If you truly wish for peace between us, it is yours," he says. "I'd rather have a dragon as an ally, than an enemy. I will draw up the agreement and we can seal it in blood."

"Good," Veron replies. "Now, let us discuss how to rid Eryadon of goblin and wolf filth."

CHAPTER 46

LYANA

We talk long into the night, explaining our journey to Caelen's family and Ruvaen. As Caelen speaks with his mentor, his father walks over to me.

"You remind me of him, you know. I will never forget how your brother stood before me and my court, demanding that we end our fighting. I thought he would make a fine ally with Dhurvaen when they both came into their rule." Sadness flits briefly across his expression. "Prince Arthur was an honorable man and a strong warrior. You honor him with your strength."

Emotions lodge in my throat, but I somehow manage to speak around them. "Thank you."

"I believe in peace." His eyes drift to Caelen, across the room. "I never imagined that the pursuit of it would bring my son so much happiness." He looks down at my hand and the ring Caelen gave me on our wedding night. The one that belonged to his wife—Caelen's mother. "If my mate were here, I believe she would have approved of your match." A faint smile quirks his lips. "Welcome to our family."

His gaze turns to Veron, who is speaking with Ruvaen. Kyvern arches a brow and he looks so much like Caelen, when he does that, I have a hard time hiding my smile. "If you will excuse me," he says, "I wish to go speak with the first dragon ever to set foot in my home."

Nurala approaches as soon as he leaves. "I overheard my father speaking with you just now."

"You were all the way across the room. How did—"

She grins and points to her ears, and we both laugh.

Her expression sobers and she takes my hand. "It is good to see my brother so happy. I hope you do not think it too forward that I already regard you as my sister."

"Of course not." I smile. "I like that."

She looks down at the ring on my hand. "Father was right. I believe our mother would have liked you." Her eyes flick up to mine. "I understand loss, Lyana. And I am sorry that you lost your family. But I want you to know that you are not alone. You are ours now just as much as you are Caelen's."

I'm moved to tears, but I push them down as she hugs me and bids me goodnight.

I step out on the balcony and into the cool night air. I gaze down at the gardens below and I'm struck by how different they are from Eryadon. Long vines with glowing white flowers hang down over the walls, swaying gently back and forth in the breeze like living curtains.

Water flows along the many pathways that wind throughout the space, weaving in and out of the many trees with rich, glowing, purple leaves. Their trunks twist at various angles, as if competing for the sun. Several flowering bushes and plants blanket the area with vibrant bioluminescent blooms of blues, reds and yellows.

Unlike Eryadon, where all the plants are trimmed and lined in perfect rows and patterns, there is a wild and unkept beauty to these gardens.

Strong arms slip around my waist from behind and pull me back against a solid wall of muscle. I tip my head back and Caelen presses a tender kiss to my forehead. "I spoke with my father," he says. "I want you to remain here. I will travel with Rivenyl's army and—"

"No." I turn in his arms to face him. "Eryadon is my kingdom by birthright. What kind of ruler would I be if I were not even present in the battle to retake it?"

He opens his mouth to protest, but I continue. "Besides, you said in each version of the future you saw in the mirror, it did not matter if I was there or not. The end"—my voice catches as I think on my demise—"you said it was the same no matter what."

Footsteps behind us draw our attention and we turn to find Ruvaen. "I believe I understand why this is," he says solemnly.

"Then, tell us," Caelen says, irritation tinging his tone. "Because I see no reason why we should not just take the chance and try to keep Lyana here, where she would be safe."

Ruvaen shakes his head. "My dear prince, there is nowhere that is safe for her. As long as she draws breath, she is a threat to the new rulers of Eryadon. They cannot allow her to live. Not if they want to ensure the hold on their reign."

"Our borders are heavily guarded and—"

"Queen Rina is a Goblin witch. She has taken the appearance of a human and deceived not only Lyana and her father, but Fredrik and the entire kingdoms of Eryadon and Winterhold. If she can take any form she desires, there is no place that she cannot infiltrate if she is determined to do so."

His words settle like a heavy stone in my gut. "He's right," I tell Caelen. "That is why the outcome does not change even if I am not present at the battle."

Ruvaen steps forward. "One thing about the visions the mirror showed you, troubles me."

"What is it?" Caelen asks.

"You are holding the apple and then you still see the glass coffin with Lyana inside." His brow furrows deeply. "There is something we are missing, but I do not know what."

His words send a chill down my spine, but I do my best to hide my fear.

Ruvaen inclines his head in a subtle bow. "I will use my magic to see what I can of the future."

"You are a seer?" I ask, taken aback. I've heard of them, but I have never met one before.

"My visions are not always clear," he explains. "And the future is always changing. Each choice we make affects the ones after."

"What do you mean?"

"Imagine standing before a pond and throwing a stone in the water. The ripples along the surface are the result of that singular event. Each of them spreading out in a different direction."

I frown. "So, how do you know which future is the correct one?"

"That is the problem," he replies. "It is why predictions of the future are so difficult to interpret in my visions." He darts a glance at Caelen. "Even so, I will divine what I can."

"Thank you, Ruvaen," I tell him.

He inclines his head. "Of course, Queen Lyana."

"You may call me Lyana," I tell him.

His lips quirk up slightly at the edges. "Thank you,

Lyana." His eyes flick to Caelen and he bows again. "I will see you both in the morning."

As soon as he's gone, Caelen wraps his arms around me. "There is always an out to any bargain," he repeats the witch's words. "We simply have to find it."

CHAPTER 47

LYANA

Caelen takes my hand as he leads me to his chambers. The entire castle is lit with floating, blue and green orbs. Their softly glowing light casts dancing shadows on the walls as we pass.

"This is beautiful," I whisper as I marvel over the ornately carved archways, columns, and corridors. The entire palace is constructed from pearlescent, white stone. Vines, flowers, and arboreal patterns are chiseled on almost every surface so perfectly they appear almost alive.

When we reach the center of the castle, I stare wide-eyed at the large atrium in the middle of the structure. A large tree bearing lovely purple, heart-shaped leaves and long, hanging vines of glowing, white flowers takes up most of the space. It is similar to the ones outside, but much larger. Around it, winding pathways cross bubbling streams that flow gently before diving beneath the stone floor to drain into one of the streams that joins the gardens outside.

Pixies flit through the atrium, landing on various yellow,

pink, and blue blossoms. The smell of roses with a slight hint of citrus fills the air. There are inviting stone benches throughout and I can just imagine myself sitting here, reading someday.

Caelen points to the tree. "It is a *sylven* apple tree. As I explained, it has always been considered a symbol of hope and life for our people. That is why my ancestors placed this one here, in the heart of the castle."

I note that some of the vines are heavily laden with apples and some only with white, glowing blossoms.

He continues. "I believe that the mirror showed me this symbol of life to convey that there is hope."

I nod, unable to speak as I think on my potential death. I dare not speak for fear that my voice will betray my fears. I do not want Caelen to know I'm afraid, because I'm already committed to this course. Whatever the risk, I cannot simply abandon my people and allow Rina and Fredrik to rule.

I have always been one to face things head on and this will not be any different. I will not hide from whatever fate has willed for me. Instead, I will meet it on my own terms. Bravely and without regret. And if I die trying to do the right thing by my kingdom and my people, it will be an honorable death.

Drawing upon the memory of my family, I push down my fears and my worries and follow Caelen as we continue through the castle.

When we reach his room, I'm surprised by how warm and inviting it is. The large fireplace in one corner is already lit, casting a soft orange glow on the walls. Thick wooden vines twist together to form a four-poster bed, with a silken canopy of sheer, pale green curtains suspended from the top. The rich, emerald comforter with a silver-threaded pattern of leaves looks so inviting. But it's the view from the balcony that takes my breath away.

Silk curtains sway gently on the cool night breeze. Hundreds of softly glowing lights below mark the enchanting city beyond. Waterfalls cascade down either side of the balcony, but I do not hear the dull roar of flowing water that I'd expect.

As if in answer to my unspoken question, Caelen says, "We use magic to dampen the noise."

I turn to him. "The treaty between Eryadon and Rivenyl, that you agreed upon with my father, bound the use of your magic while in the kingdom. How do we undo this?"

"The treaty must be torn in half to break the binding spell."

"Perhaps we could sneak into the castle and steal it and—"

His expression turns grim. "Ruvaen searched for it, in the castle library, before he escaped. Rina had already hidden it."

Pain and anger twist deep inside me at the reminder of her betrayal. "My father trusted her. Completely," I murmur. "I did too."

Caelen's strong arms envelop me as he hugs me to his chest. "I am sorry, Lyana. I cannot imagine how terrible it is to be betrayed by someone you loved."

"She was like a mother to me." My voice quavers. "I loved her so much."

He runs a hand soothingly down my back and across my shoulders. "She did not deserve you, my Lyana."

He lifts me into his arms and cradles me to his chest, carrying me to the cleansing room. "What are you doing?"

"I am taking care of you."

Before I can ask anything else, he walks us both into the cleansing room. With a snap of his fingers, the large tub is filled with water; a light mist of steam rises from the surface. Carefully, he sets me on my feet. He unfastens my dress and it falls to the floor, pooling at my feet.

Heat flushes my cheeks as Caelen's eyes travel over my

form, full of desire and longing. His gaze holds mine as he removes his clothes and then walks toward me. I stretch up on my toes to kiss him, but a surprised squeak escapes me as he puts one hand behind my back and another up under my knees, gathering me to his chest.

He walks us both into the tub. A soft sigh of contentment escapes me as we sink beneath the warm water. Caelen sits behind me, his legs on either side of mine as he pulls me back against him.

"This is bliss," I whisper as I allow my head to fall back against his broad, muscular chest.

"I agree," he murmurs into my hair. "We could stay here forever, you know."

It is a lovely dream, to imagine that we have nothing left to do but live out our lives like this. But I cannot abandon my throne and my people. "Caelen, I—"

"I know," he whispers solemnly. He cups my chin and turns my head just enough to look back at him. "I have one request before we go into battle."

"What is it?"

"Stay close to the dragon. You will be safer with him."

"What about you?"

"I must lead Rivenyl's army." He pauses. "We will discuss it with Veron tomorrow, when we meet with the Dwarves."

While I understand that I'm not a warrior, I am not useless either. "I can fight, Caelen. I have had training with a bow and arrow. And while I know it is not much, it is still something."

"All the more reason you should be with the dragon. On the ground, it will be sword, axe, and shield on the battleground. In the air, you can use the skills for which you have been training." He pauses. "Or perhaps you could remain in the mountain with the Dwarves while—"

"No, Caelen," I state firmly. "We've already been through this. I will not stay behind and ask others to fight for me."

He brushes the hair back from my face and narrows his eyes. "Why did the gods curse me with such a brave, but stubborn mate?"

I laugh softly. "Oh," I tease, as I straighten and grab the edge of the tub, starting to pull myself out of the water. "If you consider it a curse to be mated to me, perhaps I should just find another room, and sleep elsewhere tonight and—"

Before I can finish my sentence, he grabs me so quickly, I let out a surprised gasp as he pulls me back down to him. He turns me in his arms to face him, my thighs straddling his hips.

He slips his strong arms around my back and pulls me so close there is no space between our bodies. His stav is a hard bar between us as he stares up at me, his gaze intense. "You are staying right here," he says, hoarse with arousal.

I open my mouth to offer another teasing reply, but he crushes his mouth to mine in a searing kiss, stealing the breath from my lungs.

He positions himself at my entrance. My head falls back and a soft moan escapes my lips as he slowly enters me.

The deep stretch of my body as his stav fills my channel is the most exquisite pleasure as he begins to stroke up into me. His knot expands and it isn't long before I'm falling over the edge into blissful oblivion, crying out his name as I find my release.

My climax triggers his own. He roars my name as he erupts deep within. Intense warmth floods my channel as he fills me with his seed.

I'm breathless and panting as he lifts us out of the water. He wraps a towel loosely around his hips as he carefully dries me off and then slips a silken sleep gown over my body. The material is softer than anything I've ever felt before.

Caelen carries me to the bed and crawls in beside me. He pulls me into his arms, and seals his mouth over mine in a passionate kiss.

His fingers trace down my thigh and he cups the back of my knee, pulling it over his hips. His stav is hard against the entrance to my core.

"You want me again so soon?"

"I always want you," he whispers between kisses. "Will you take me?"

"Yes," I smile against his lips.

Without hesitation, he rolls me beneath him, his gaze full of possession. He slices a line down the fabric of my night-dress with his claws, baring me to his gaze.

I purse my lips. "You know, this is the second sleeping gown you've ruined."

"I'll have more made for you," he says, as he lowers his head and traces his tongue over my already sensitive flesh.

I arch up into him and a low growl vibrates in his chest. He rises up and positions himself at my entrance. His gaze holds mine as he sinks deep inside me. Each stroke of his body into mine is longer and deeper than the last.

When I reach my climax, we fall over the edge together into blissful oblivion. He's still knotted inside me when he rolls us onto our sides, holding me close against his chest. I love being connected like this to him.

"Sleep, my Lyana," he breathes in my ear.

As I drift away, he whispers words in the Elvish tongue that, although I do not know their translation, I understand they are words of love and devotion.

CHAPTER 48

CAELEN

My father has sent Rivenyl's army to march toward Eryadon. It will take them two days to arrive, where I will join them in the attack.

The trip to the Dwarves' mountain has been much shorter than I expected. Although Lyana is my mate, I dread seeing her friend, Bran, again. His feelings about both her and me were made very clear when last we saw him.

I anticipate a fight, or at the very least, an argument. He is more likely to believe I've cast a spell of enchantment upon her rather than that she is actually in love with me.

Regardless, I know he cares for her, and that is the most important thing. They all do. If this goes bad, I have no doubt the Dwarves will protect her, defending her to their last breath.

As Veron circles the mountain, I'm surprised the Dwarves appear unafraid. The sight of a dragon should be more than enough to send them scrambling. Perhaps they are as dull-witted as my people believe them to be.

Even as I think this, a pang of guilt stabs through me. They are good people who took us in when we needed help most. They could have cast me out immediately, while Lyana was unconscious, but they did not.

Veron dips his wing, and the moment they see Lyana, every Dwarf stops to wave. They stare gaping as we land. King Edwyrd rushes toward us, his face bright red as he waves his staff.

"How dare you show up like this unannounced? On the back of a dragon, no less?"

Veron shifts into his two-legged form, crossing his arms and pursing his lips, appearing slightly irritated.

"I—" Lyana starts to explain, but I step between her and the king. I level an angry glare at him, growling low.

He huffs out an annoyed breath. "Calm down, Elf. I merely jest." He pushes past me and gathers Lyana in his arms, hugging her warmly. "We've been so worried for you since you left."

She hugs him in return. "I'm sorry. There was no way to send word."

As he spins her around, I do not miss the way he eyes *me* with distrust.

Not the fire-breathing dragon standing beside us. *Me.*

He narrows his eyes. "I see you're still keeping company with the High Elves."

"Really?" I ask emphatically. I gesture to Veron. "There is a dragon in your midst, and *I'm* the bigger concern here?"

The king's eyes shift to Veron and then back to me. "Aye. Everyone knows that *there* is a changed dragon. Changed by love, in fact. He has come to us many times to mold gold or silver into gifts for his human mate."

Ah. Now I understand why they were unafraid. They know him.

"Caelen is my husband," Lyana states firmly. "He's good to me, and I love him."

Something freezes at the edge of my vision. Bran's mouth falls open. "You love him?" he demands.

"Yes."

"I knew it!" Bran exclaims. "He's spelled you, hasn't he?"

"No, Bran, he has not," she states firmly. "Besides, you know the treaty his people have with Eryadon prevents them from using magic within Eryadon's borders."

He looks down, brows furrowed in deep contemplation. After a moment, he heaves a sigh and joins us. He places a hand on each of our shoulders and gives me a threatening glare. "Be good to her, or it's the axe for your head, Elf."

Lyana and Bran laugh, but the glint in his eye tells me his threat has substance. I've no doubt he would not hesitate to end me if he thought I was mistreating her.

I wrap an arm around her waist and pull her close. "I would sooner take my own life than ever hurt her."

"Good," he says. "Now, tell me why you're here with the dragon."

King Edwyrd steps forward, studying me with a look I cannot quite discern. "Will your people help retake Eryadon, or have you come alone?"

"Rivenyl's forces arrive in two days."

"Good," he says. "We'll need them. Fredrik's father sent more men from Winterhold, doubling their numbers. They mean to hang onto this kingdom, fang and claw."

Panic twists deep inside me as the images from the mirror return.

CHAPTER 49

LYANA

As Bran listens to our story, his eyes widen when Caelen tells him about the vision of my death in the mirror's foretelling. His head snaps to me. "You're not going into battle. You will stay here in the mountain, where it's safe."

"No, I am not," I state firmly. "I will not ask others to fight a war for me that I, myself, will not even fight. I would never do that."

"Kings do it all the time," Bran counters. "They send their armies to war and receive reports on the progress back in the comfort of their castles."

"That's not the kind of ruler I wish to be," I snap.

Bran jerks his head to Caelen. "And you're telling me that you are all right with this? *You*, who claim to love her?"

"What would you have me do?" Caelen asks. "Bind her in chains to keep her away from battle?"

"Yes," Bran says. "If that's what it takes."

Anger roils through me. "You demand that Caelen treat

me well, but then suggest that he should hold me against my will because I want to go into battle?"

"The visions in the mirror showed you lying in a glass coffin, Lyana." Bran runs a hand roughly through his hair. "I don't understand. Do you want to die?"

My breath catches as the terrible image fills my mind. "No." I lower my gaze, not wanting him to see the tears in my eyes. "But Caelen also saw the *sylven* apple. It's a symbol of hope and life and—"

"I doubt all the apples in the world will matter if you suffer a wound from an arrow through the heart, a sword that's run you through or an axe that's cut you in half," Bran counters. "You cannot pin your hopes on a symbol, Lyana."

"I'll be wearing armor," I tell him. "Caelen brought armor for me to—"

"Perhaps that is the problem," he huffs. His gaze slides to Caelen. "Maybe that's the bit you were supposed to pay attention to so as to avoid a dire fate. Everyone knows Elvish armor is inferior to the stuff we make here. Follow me. Bring your armor as well, Elf."

"Why?" Caelen asks, indignant.

Bran rolls his eyes. "I'll have my brother reinforce it with Dwarvish steel to strengthen it. I'll not have you dying out there on the battlefield and leaving my best friend a sobbing widow."

CHAPTER 50

CAELEN

I'm actually surprised that he cares about my well-being. I'd have thought he would want me gone so he could—

He places a hand on my shoulder and meets my gaze evenly. "I can see the wheels spinning in your mind, and I know what you're thinking."

I arch a brow. "Oh, so now Dwarves are mind readers, are they?"

He shakes his head. "No, but if I were you, I'd be thinking the same. Just so you know... as long as she's happy, so am I. And I'd like to keep it that way."

I stare at him in astonishment, not sure how to respond.

"Before you say anything, Elf, this *does not* make us friends."

Despite his words, I notice the slight quirk of his lips at the edges. "Of course not," I reply. "But, thank you, none-theless."

He dips his chin in a subtle nod.

Bran leads us deeper into the mountain. I'm still astonished by how bright it is in here. Before we came here the first time, I had never been inside a Dwarf stronghold. I always assumed their homes were dark and damp, but I was wrong. Glowing gemstones embedded in the walls light up the spaces as brightly as if there were windows allowing in the sun.

I marvel at how precisely carved each stone is within these halls. All of it master craftsmanship. The Dwarves are able to whisper to stones to position them as they wish, but these intricate carvings are all done by hand.

He leads us to a forge. A dwarf hammers at a sword before carefully lifting it with tongs and plunging it into a bucket of cold water. Soot streaks his leather apron and brawny forearms, while his forehead drips with sweat.

As we approach, a bright smile lights his face and he drops everything to rush to Lyana. He lifts her up, spinning her around in a hug that stirs irrational jealousy deep within me. These Dwarves are far more familiar with my mate than I like.

When he sets her back down, she introduces us. "Tomys, this is my husband, Caelen. Caelen, Tomys."

Tomys's face falls and he narrows his eyes. "This is the Elf you wed?"

She nods.

He steps closer, his eyes locked on mine. Only now do I see the resemblance. He looks so much like Bran, I would have known they are brothers without being told. "I didn't get a good look at you when you were here last," he grumbles as he studies me with a piercing gaze. After a moment, he turns to Lyana. "Are you happy with this one?" He gestures to me as if I were not even here.

A smile tilts her lips. "More than I could have ever imagined."

All my anger disappears at her words, but it quickly returns when Tomys looks to me. "I'll let him live then, and I'll pray the old gods look favorably upon you when your children are born that they take after their mother."

A growl rises in my throat, but I stop when Lyana takes my hand and flashes a gorgeous smile at me. "Oh, Caelen, he's merely teasing, my love."

One look at the Dwarf tells me his words were not entirely made in jest, but I decide to let it go. These Dwarves are protective of my mate and I cannot fault them for their devotion to her.

"They need their armor strengthened," Bran says, changing the subject.

I hand him two bags with our armor.

He rummages through it and holds up a breastplate, studying it intently. "It's actually not too bad," he admits.

High praise from a Dwarf.

He continues. "Just a bit of reinforcing should do the trick."

"Will you have to melt it down?" I ask, wondering how long this process will take. Tomorrow, Rivenyl's army will arrive at Eryadon castle. We do not have much time.

He shakes his head and carries the pieces to a cauldron where molten metal bubbles. I suck in a quick breath as he throws the armor in and begins to whisper words that must be enchantments.

When he finishes, he carefully fishes the components out with tongs and lays them on the table. The shape and engravings appear the same, but the metal has a bit of a grayish tinge to it, instead of the green that marks the armor of my people. "What did you do?"

"We do not simply whisper to stones, Elf Prince. Metal listens to us too."

I blink several times, astonished. I'd never heard the Dwarves were able to do this.

I pick up a greave, surprised that the weight has somehow not changed despite the new reinforcing. "Magic," I whisper, more to myself than to him.

"More like an agreement between us and the earth," he says.

He hands the pieces to Lyana, asking her to try them on. She puts them over her clothing and he speaks additional words of enchantment. I watch as it conforms to her perfectly. Next, he hands her an expertly crafted bow.

She takes it in her hands, testing the weight. She pulls back the drawstring and then smiles brightly at him. "Thank you, Tomys. Everything is perfect."

His cheeks flush bright red as she gives him a quick peck on the cheek. He turns his attention to me as I extend my arm and he takes it. "Thank you," I tell him. "Truly."

"Just keep her safe," he says. "That's all that we ask."

My gaze sweeps over him and the rest of the Dwarves that have gathered around us, each studying me intently. "With my life," I vow.

CHAPTER 51

LYANA

As we lie in bed, Caelen slips his arms around my waist and tugs me to him. I nestle even further into his chest, resting my head on his shoulder. "They all love you," he whispers, and I realize he is speaking of the Dwarves. "I'd always heard they were like dragons. Incapable of loving anything but gold, silver, and gemstones, but it seems I was wrong," he muses. A smile tugs at his lips. "They tolerate me, but only for your sake."

I laugh, because it's true. "Are you not the same toward them, my love?"

"I suppose you are right," he chuckles. His expression sobers and he nuzzles my hair. "Promise me you'll stay with Veron."

"I promise."

He holds me until my eyes will no longer remain open and I fall into a fitful sleep.

When morning comes, Caelen and I both dress. Neither of us slept much last night. In fact, I doubt he slept at all, judging by the dark circles under his eyes.

He looks so fierce and handsome in his Elvish armor. Like a warrior king of old. He tightens the straps of my armor, making sure it is secure. My heart melts as he goes over it once more after that.

As we stand with King Edwyrd, I allow my gaze to travel over the Dwarves, armored and ready for battle. My heart clenches because I know they do this more for me than anything else.

They could easily keep to their mountain and I doubt Fredrik or Rina would bother them. Instead, they choose to go to war to help me retake my throne and my kingdom. I think on my death foretold by the mirror and only pray that I live long enough to see victory.

I do not want the Dwarves to be left to the mercy of Fredrik and Rina after I'm gone.

King Edwyrd addresses his men and then they begin to march toward the castle. He turns to me, taking my hand. "Your parents would be proud of you. You honor them today. Remember that."

I swallow against the lump in my throat. "Thank you. And... thank you for coming to my aid when I need you."

He dips his chin. "We owe you our lives. We'd have starved if not for you. The people remember and they love you for it." He turns to Caelen, who is observing us from off to the side. He claps a hand on his shoulder. "You, on the other hand, are a bit of a hard sell," he teases. "Fortunately for you, Lyana has vouched for you with our people."

A smile tugs at Caelen's mouth as he nods.

King Edwyrd mounts his horse and leaves to join his men.

Veron stands behind us in his dragon form, waiting.

Caelen gathers me to his chest and crushes his lips to mine in a fiery kiss. When he pulls back, he cups my chin and drops his forehead gently to my own. "You are my heart, Lyana. Whatever happens today, I want you to promise me that you'll not risk yourself, no matter what."

"I will be careful," I promise.

A knot of dread twists deep inside me, but I push it back down, not wanting him to see my fear.

He kisses me again; this time tender and slow. When he pulls back, he touches my face, staring at me with a strange mixture of worry and devotion. "Remember your promise. Stay with Veron. No matter what happens, Lyana."

"I will," I whisper softly. "Be careful, my love."

He presses another tender kiss to my lips before he returns to his horse and leaves to join his army.

I draw in a deep and steeling breath as I turn to Veron and climb onto his back. "Hold tightly to me, my Queen," his voice rumbles low. "I plan on both of us surviving this day."

"So do I."

CHAPTER 52

CAELEN

As we approach the castle, Eryadon's forces are a solid wall between us and the castle. They believe us to be an invading force.

Rumors that me and my people killed their former king and that I stole the princess have been spread far and wide. Winterhold's army stands behind them. Together, their numbers are equal to us and the Dwarves.

A great field lies between us, pristine green grass and various flowering plants dot its landscape. Before this day is over, it will be covered in blood and fallen soldiers.

Prince Fredrik sits on his horse on the front line, readying to give the order to charge as we stare at each other across the battlefield.

King Edwyrd rides at the head of his men as they approach. His army stops and I watch as he moves out toward the middle of the field and stops. "Soldiers of Eryadon!" he calls out. "Long have our people been allies and friends. I come before you now to tell you the truth. Your queen is not who she says she is. She is a Goblin witch disguised as a human. She and her lover, Prince Fredrik of Winterhold are the ones responsible for the death of your king."

"Lies!" a voice calls out from across the way.

"It is truth!" Edwyrd replies. "Your princess was saved by her Elven husband. Rivenyl is not your enemy and neither am I."

Fredrik raises his sword, ready to give the command to charge when a thunderous roar fills the air.

Their heads whip toward the sky and they stare gaping as Veron flies overhead. He swoops down low and releases another bellowing roar. He dips his left wing to reveal Lyana atop his shoulders, dressed from head to toe in her armor with a bow and arrows strung across her back.

"Soldiers of Eryadon!" she cries out. "Your queen has deceived you! She and her lover—Prince Fredrik—betrayed your rightful king—my father—to his death and would have sent me to mine if I had not escaped with my husband!"

I observe as several Eryadon soldiers level dark glares at Fredrik, atop his horse.

She continues. "I have come with the Dragon of Eryadon, the Dwarven army of the Nylrian and Ferylan Mountains, and the Elven army of Rivenyl to take back what is mine! Which of you will follow your rightful queen and deliver Eryadon from the hands of her enemies?"

As one, the soldiers of Eryadon raise their swords to Lyana.

Veron releases another rage-filled roar, shaking the ground beneath us.

"I call for revenge for the death of my father!" Lyana cries out. "I call upon every true soldier of Eryadon to drive out the invaders who would try to take out lands!"

One of Eryadon's captains releases a battle cry and

charges toward Fredrik. The others follow suit, attacking the soldiers of Winterhold.

Undeterred, Fredrik raises his arm and emits a war cry, urging his guards to attack.

His men rush toward us.

King Edwyrd and I exchange a look, and then charge forward with our armies.

The ground shakes as galloping hooves thunder across the earth and men release battle cries in a cacophony of noise.

Veron swoops down low, releasing a stream of fire along the back of Fredrik's ranks. Screams of agony echo across the fields.

Queen Rina orders archers on the wall to target him, but everyone knows regular weapons do not work on dragons. Only those forged of *L'omhara* can pierce his thick scales, and Lyana said Eryadon had few of these in supply.

Veron spreads his wings wide, twisting at the last second to take the rain of arrows, shielding my mate from any harm. I watch in triumph as they bounce harmlessly off his scales.

It seems the queen's archers either have not found the right arrows, or have yet to use them.

I'm hoping it's the former.

As we approach, Fredrik's men crouch in battle formation, shields up and spears out. I lean forward and swing my sword in a wide arc, pushing away and breaking several of their spears as my steed charges through their line.

I turn just as one of the men shifts into his *Wolven* form. He barrels into my side, throwing me from my horse. Before I've even landed, he wraps his arms around me, snapping his massive jaws at my face. I twist, narrowly missing his sharp fangs, and plunge my sword deep into his chest.

I jump to my feet and another attacks. We tumble to the

ground in a tangled mess of limbs, each of us trying to pin the other beneath them.

My heart pounds as I slam my fist against his chest, forcing him back, only to have him replaced by yet another Wolf.

I extend my nails into sharp claws, and rake them across his throat. A spray of dark blood splashes my face and armor, but I swipe it away as I attack the next one.

Panting heavily, I surge to my feet after I take down another. My armor, I note, appears undamaged. The Dwarvish steel is much stronger than I'd expected.

Taking advantage of a momentary break, I cast my gaze to the sky and watch as Lyana launches an arrow and the dragon shoots fire toward the queen.

Rina throws up a shield of magic, protecting herself from the flame and the arrows.

A deep rumbling growl forces my attention back to my own battle as another Wolf hurtles toward me. I swing my sword in a wide arc, cutting through his chest.

Veron swoops low and opens his mouth, releasing a torrent of flame on the ground between the army of Winterhold and the castle, cutting them off if they dare try to retreat behind its heavily fortified walls.

A lone figure appears on the outer wall, staring out at the battle. I recognize Queen Rina immediately as she moves to a new position. She raises her arms and sends a blast of wind toward the flames, smothering them quickly.

With the use of so much magic, she is unable to hide her true form. I observe as it falls away to reveal the Goblin beneath. With lavender skin and long purple hair. She holds up her hands, gathering a glowing red orb of magic between them, readying to cast again.

Fredrik appears so shocked that he drops his sword. It is

just as the witch in the cottage told us. He did not know his lover was a Goblin.

With her disguise gone, so is her heavily swollen abdomen. Rina was never with child as she claimed.

Fredrik shifts instantly into a massive dark brown Wolf. He releases a piercing howl, stopping all his men in their tracks as they turn to him. "We have been deceived!" he cries out. "Kill her! Kill the Queen!"

"No!" Rina calls to him. "Stop!"

"My kind will not fight and shed blood to defend a Goblin witch!" he yells.

She throws her hands, sending the orb spiraling toward him.

Fredrik leaps out of the way, but not quick enough. It catches his side, sending him sprawling.

"Save the Prince!" several of his men call out.

A few of them rush toward him. Gathering him in their arms, they place him on a horse and spirit him away, while the rest continue to charge toward the castle.

Rina throws up a shield as Veron flies low and releases another stream of flame directly over her.

Her arms shake from so much use of her magic. It is only a matter of time before she will be too weak to cast.

Her eyes are wide as she struggles to hold her protective shield intact.

I observe as her image flickers and distorts a moment before reappearing. It seems she is too weak to transport herself away from here as well.

Veron lands close to her, on the wall. Lyana slides from his back and approaches. "Surrender now or you will be shown no mercy."

Rina drops the shield of magic around her and raises her hands. "I surrender!"

CHAPTER 53

CAELEN

Several of the guards surround Rina and march her down to the courtyard.

I rush toward Lyana. Gathering her in my arms, I spin her around once as I hug her close to my chest before pressing a tender kiss to her head and setting her feet back on the ground.

"Are you hurt?" Her eyes rake over the blood that covers my face and armor.

"No. I am fine."

Over her shoulder, I'm acutely aware of Rina's reptilian amber eyes watching us closely as she remains surrounded by the guards.

Lyana takes my hand, squeezing it gently before she releases it and turns her attention back to Rina.

"What would you have us do with her, my queen?" one of the guards asks Lyana.

"Take her to the dungeons. We will decide her fate later."

One of them grabs Rina's arm and drags her to her feet.

JESSICA GRAYSON & ARIA WINTER

"Wait!" she calls out. "I wish to say something."

Lyana's eyes snap to her. "What is it?"

"You turned Fredrik against me," she says, tears of anger sliding down her cheeks. "The only man I ever truly loved."

"You killed my father and betrayed my love for you, *Stepmother*," Lyana grinds out. "You are lucky you still draw breath."

"Am I?" Rina tips up her chin in defiance. "You took from me the one that I love and now I will take yours from you."

Rina closes her eyes and my heart stops as she whispers words of enchantment. Light gathers around her and the world shifts into slow motion, as I realize too late that it was all a ruse.

Her magic was never weakening. This was her plan all along.

Her eyes snap open and she raises her hands. Magic explodes like fire from her fingers and arcs toward me.

I cannot move fast enough as the blast races toward me. Raising my hands in futility, I cry out in panic as Lyana throws herself at me, pushing me out of the way.

Sacrificing herself, I watch in horror as she takes the full brunt of the blast. She cries out in pain as it slams into her side, pushing her into my arms as she collapses against me.

Veron roars and releases a ball of flame. Rina's piercing shriek fills the air a moment before falling silent as he burns her to ash.

I stare down at Lyana's pale and trembling form. Without hesitation, I bite my wrist to draw blood and place it over her mouth. "Drink," I tell her. "It will heal you."

She does as I ask. The color returns to her cheeks, but she begins shivering. Her face is an agonizing mask of pain as she stares up at me. Tightly gripping the sleeve of my forearm, her chest rises and falls with rapid breaths as tears stream down her cheeks.

Ruvaen drops to his knees by my side. "I don't understand," I tell him. "I gave her my blood. Why is she not recovering?"

I quickly pull off her armor and rip a line down her tunic to expose her injury. My heart stops as my gaze travels over the angry red veins fingering out from the wound.

Ruvaen inhales sharply. "Poisonous magic," he whispers in disbelief. "I—I have heard of this, but I have never seen it."

Sweat beads across Lyana's forehead and her skin is fever warm to the touch as the poison burns through her veins.

Frantic, I look to him. "Help her!" I demand.

He stares down at her in shock. "There is nothing I can do, Caelen."

Her small hand reaches up to cup my cheek. I lower my forehead gently to hers. "Please, Lyana, you must hold on, my beloved."

Golden-brown eyes stare into mine as she whispers. "I love you, Caelen."

"Lyana, I—"

My heart stops as her eyes close and her hand falls from my face as she goes still. I cup the back of her neck and her long, dark hair spills through my fingers. "Lyana," I whisper, but she does not respond.

Raw pain tears through me as I realize she will open her beautiful eyes no more. I gather her to my chest and roar my anguish to the sky.

CHAPTER 54

CAELEN

I stand before the glass coffin that holds my beloved. Dressed in a long, silken, blue gown, she appears as if she is only sleeping. I struggle to blink back tears as I place my hand atop hers.

Even in death, her cheeks and lips still hold their color. Bran stands on the other side of her, his entire face a mask of pain. "It is only a curse," he murmurs. "It must be."

I clench my jaw, unable to speak, praying he is right.

We sent word to the Fae Kingdom of Anara. Their Healer —Oradon—is familiar with cursed and poisoned magic, according to Ruvaen.

"Healer Oradon will be here soon," I tell him. "The dragon should be back with him anytime now."

Closing my eyes, I send a silent prayer to the old gods.

Healer Oradon is our last hope.

The heavy thud of booted steps draws my attention and I turn to find Oradon walking toward us. His glowing blue eyes widen as he looks beyond me to Lyana.

Prince Ryvan and his human mate, Princess Ella, are only a few steps behind him. I did not expect them to come. Especially when I notice her swollen abdomen—heavy with their child.

Although it has been many years since we've seen each other, Ryvan and Oradon greet me warmly. "Caelen, I am so sorry." Ryvan's glowing green eyes search mine in concern, his clear membranous wings fluttering behind him. "We would have come sooner if—"

"It is all right," I tell him.

Over his shoulder, I notice Veron. I dip my chin in a subtle thanks to the dragon for having brought them here so quickly. He does the same in return.

Envy fills me as his mate—Alara—rushes to him. He pulls her into a warm embrace. I think of Lyana and the last time I held her like that.

I turn my attention back to Ryvan. He runs a hand roughly through his short dark hair as his wings flutter behind him. He gestures to his human mate. Her long, brown hair is braided down her back and her sky-blue eyes stare up at me with a pitying look. "This is my mate, Princess Ella."

"How long has she been like this?" Ella asks.

"Two days," I answer, struggling to keep my voice from breaking as sadness tears at my heart.

Oradon moves to Lyana's side and carefully studies her. He bows his head and begins speaking words of enchantment.

My jaw drops and Bran inhales sharply as a soft, red glow surrounds Lyana's body.

"What is that?" I ask.

"Ruvaen was right," Oradon murmurs. "It is a poisoned curse."

"How do we break it?"

He looks to me. "Tell me about your visions. Ruvaen's letter said something about a sylven apple."

"Yes. In every vision granted to me by the mirror, I saw the dragon, the apple and Lyana in a glass coffin."

Ruvaen moves to my side and addresses Oradon. "Sylven apples are a symbol of hope and life in our kingdom. It is the same in yours, is it not?"

"Yes."

"I thought the apple was a symbol," I explain. "I thought the mirror showed it to me to give us hope that she could be saved. I—" My voice hitches as I look at Lyana's still form. "I foolishly thought it was a good omen."

"It is," Oradon says. "Before the Great Wars, it was rather common for our kind and yours to take humans as their mates. There are stories of not only extending their lives by marking them with our dark kiss, but also of healing them with the nectar of sylven apple blossoms when they became injured or ill."

Hope fills me. "I can send for—"

"There is no need," he says. "I brought some with me." He holds up a small vial of liquid. "I carry it with me at all times in case Princess Ella needs it."

"And you believe it will break the curse?" Ruvaen asks.

He shakes his head. "Not on its own."

"What do you mean?" I ask. "What else must be done?"

"A poisoned curse requires an antidote"—he holds up the vial—"and a counter spell."

"What is the counter spell?"

"True love's kiss," he replies. "You must pour a few drops of the liquid in her mouth and then kiss her. The tonic will counter the effects of the poison, but only something as strong and powerful as love will break the curse."

I take the vial from Oradon. I gaze down at my mate. Her

long, black hair is spread out beneath her like a beautiful halo. Long, dark lashes fan across soft, pink cheeks. Her lips are parted in a small *o*.

I reach down and gently cup her face, tracing my thumb across her petal-soft skin.

Everyone stands behind me, observing silently as I pour three drops of the liquid in her mouth.

I lean down and press my lips to hers in a tender kiss. A tear slips down my cheek as I take her hand in mine and whisper. "I love you. Come back to me, my Lyana."

I hold my breath, watching her closely, praying to see the rise and fall of her chest, but nothing happens.

Panic and devastation war within me, threatening to lay waste to my already fragile control.

Lyana's eyes flutter softly.

"Lyana?" I barely manage, my heart pounding.

Her golden-brown eyes open and she gives me a faint smile. "Caelen?" she murmurs. "What happened?"

Emotions lodge in my throat and I'm unable to speak. Tears sting my eyes as her gaze holds mine.

"Caelen, what is wrong?"

I pull her into my arms, holding her close to my chest. "I thought I had lost you," I barely manage. "The witch cursed you and I thought—" My voice catches, and I cannot push the words past my lips.

"Caelen." She looks down, only now noticing the glass coffin. When she lifts her gaze, she cups my cheek. "You did it." She smiles. "You found a way to save me."

Unable to speak, I nod. I'm so relieved she's awake, I cannot stop touching her. I press a series of kisses to her forehead, cheeks, brow and nose before claiming her mouth in a tender kiss. When I pull back, I drop my forehead gently to hers.

"I love you, Caelen," she whispers softly.

I brush my lips to hers and whisper against them. "Ashal'veh, my Lyana."

CHAPTER 55

CAELEN

Lyana stands before me in a simple, white gown. Her long, black hair is tied in a series of intricate braids atop her head, twisting into a lovely crown. A few stray locks frame her heart-shaped face. Her pale skin glows beneath the light of the Hunter's Moon.

Our friends and family surround us, standing witness to our Elven ceremony. Her golden-brown eyes never leave mine as she recites the ancient vows of bonding.

"You are my heart," she whispers, "and I am yours."

"You are my heart," I repeat, "and I am yours."

I pull her into my arms and kiss her passionately. When we separate, she beams, and my heart clenches.

I touch her cheek, and whisper softly. "Are you happy, my Lyana?"

She kisses me again and then smiles. "More than words can say."

At our reception, Bran, his brothers, and his father offer congratulations to Lyana and thinly veiled threats to lop off my head with an axe if I ever mistreat her. A smile tugs at Bran's mouth as he claps me on the shoulder. "I suppose we'll have to be friends now, you and I."

I arch a teasing brow in return. "I suppose you are right."

Halla and Gerold hug her close. Errik grins as his glowing, blue eyes meet mine. "A High Elf for a cousin," he muses. "What other Mer can claim such a thing?"

I laugh. "Only you, I suspect."

Veron and Alara wish us joy. Alara hugging each of us while Veron offers me his arm in friendship.

Ryvan wishes us many blessings and Ella hugs Lyana in a warm embrace. "You will have to come visit us soon," she tells my mate.

Ryvan looks to me and I nod. "We will be sure to do that," I promise.

Tears gather in the corner of my eyes as Ruvaen and my sister—Nurala—embrace Lyana warmly. My father follows their lead. It warms my heart to know they have accepted her fully into our family.

Nurala takes Lyana's hand and my father grabs my arm. It is tradition, but I find that I do not want it as they draw us apart. I cling to Lyana's hand, not wanting to let go just yet.

My sister smiles. "You'll see her in a bit during the Hunt, Caelen."

Reluctantly, I release her.

CHAPTER 56

LYANA

Caelen's sister paints my face and exposed skin with the markings of the Wild Hunt. Anticipation quickens my pulse as Nurala paints a fertility symbol across my lower abdomen. To think that once I was afraid of this. Now, my heart pounds in anticipation of being caught by my mate and ravished beneath the stars.

I peer at the sky. The silver light of the Hunter's Moon beams overhead.

"The gods shine down upon your union," she says. Gently, she squeezes my hands. "Go to the woods."

According to Nurala, this part of the forest is much older than the one that surrounds the castle. The thick branches are heavily laden with glowing purple, heart-shaped leaves and flowing vines of softly, glowing white flowers wrapped around thick trunks and suspended from their boughs, swaying back and forth on the breeze.

A thick blanket of pale, glowing green moss covers the

forest floor. It's soft and spongy beneath my bare feet. The air is cool and crisp. The silken green dress only goes to mid-thigh and I'm completely bare underneath, as is the custom.

I pause. "How will I find Caelen?"

She grins. "*He* will find you."

She hugs me once more and then heads back to the castle.

As I pick my way through the forest, wiry branches and thick leaves snag my dress as if trying to ensnare me for my husband. I tug at the fabric, tearing free.

The sound of footsteps racing toward me draws my attention, and my heart begins to tap out a frantic beat.

I turn and bolt in the opposite direction. A deep rumbling growl echoes behind me, lending speed to my steps as I race away from my husband—the Hunter.

This is all part of the chase—the Wild Hunt—that he told me about. Even so, nervous anticipation fills me as I rush through the woods.

I look back, but stop abruptly as I bump against something solid. I turn and find myself directly against Caelen. His gaze is feral as his green eyes rake over me, full of desire and hunger.

His lips pull back, baring his fangs as he lifts a strand of hair, allowing the silken lock to slip through his lethal claws.

"Give yourself to me." He looms overhead, the silver light and shadows sculpting the thick cords of muscle that line his bare chest and abdomen. The symbols painted on his skin glow softly in the dark as his gleaming eyes lock onto mine. My heart stutters and stops as he stares down at me, fiercely handsome and lethal all at once. "You are mine," he growls, "and I will claim you."

"No!" I smack his hand away and rush in the opposite direction, as is expected during the chase.

The Wild Hunt is not meant to be won easily.

He races after me, jumping to block my path. I dart to the side, dodging him over and over again. He is faster than I am and I know he could easily catch me if he wanted, but this is all part of the ritual.

The longer the chase, the sweeter the surrender.

I dash away again and stumble into the middle of a clearing. The moon is bright above us, bathing the field in silver light.

Caelen stalks toward me, his chin lowered as he stares at me intensely. "Give yourself to me," he rumbles. "You are mine, and I will claim you this night, beneath the light of the Hunter's moon."

He stops before me. I glance down behind him and notice a blanket spread out upon the ground. My pulse pounds between my thighs. This was all part of his plan. He chased me here so he could take me beneath the full light of the moon.

His chest rises and falls. My gaze travels over the painted markings of the Hunt across his bare chest and abdomen. Desire pools deep in my core as I recognize the same fertility symbol just barely visible above the waistband of his pants.

I raise my hand to bat him away, but he catches my wrist, trapping me. He moves behind me and wraps his arm tightly around my waist, pulling me back into the solid wall of his chest. He places a hand on my chin, tilting my head to one side as he scents my neck.

His breath is warm in my ear as he whispers, "Your scent calls to me, my beloved. I long to bind you to me: body, mind, heart, and soul. Tell me: Do you surrender? Will you take me as yours?" He dips his head to the curve of my collar. His sharp fangs graze across the thin skin over my artery. "Will you bind yourself to me in all ways?"

I am already bound to this man. I have been from the

moment he gave me a choice, the day he offered me his blade in the throne room. And now, he offers another choice.

A shiver runs through me, not from fear but pleasure. My voice comes out barely a whisper. "Yes."

I'm breathless with anticipation as he extends his claws and slices a line down the front of my dress, then slides the fabric off me.

He cups my breast, rolling the hard tip between his thumb and forefinger as he laves his tongue across the sensitive skin of my neck. His stav is hard against my backside.

Pleasure coils tight inside me as he turns me in his arms to face him and bears me to the ground. His lips and tongue are everywhere as he hovers over my body, worshipping me beneath the light of the Hunter's Moon.

He parts my legs and dips his head between them, dragging his tongue through my already slick folds. "Your body is fertile," he rasps. His emerald green eyes lock onto mine, a question behind them.

I touch his face, and he leans into my palm. "I want everything with you, my love."

Desire burns in his gaze as he lowers his head back between my thighs. I writhe beneath his attention, threading my fingers through his hair to hold him in place as he concentrates his attention on the small pearl of flesh that drives my desire even higher.

He growls as I dig my heels into his back and arch against his mouth. My entire body goes taut like a bowstring before I cry his name to the stars as I find my release.

I'm breathless and panting as Caelen moves back up my body. He notches his stav to my entrance. He grips my chin, forcing my gaze to his. His eyes never leave mine, and my breathing catches at the delicious stretch as he slowly enters, filling me completely.

A soft moan escapes my lips as he sheathes himself deep

inside me. He wraps his hand around my thigh, adjusting the angle of his hips and groans as he sinks impossibly deeper.

He stills and touches my cheek, tenderly stroking his thumb across my skin as he stares down at me, full of love and devotion. "You are my heart," he whispers.

"And you are mine," I reply.

He begins a slow and steady rhythm as he strokes deep inside me. I moan at the delicious friction of his stav in my channel. My inner muscles flex and quiver around his length as I draw closer to the edge.

He clenches his jaw, "So tight," he rasps.

He runs his hand through my hair, gripping the dark strands between his fingers as he tips my head to the side, baring my neck. His fangs extend and sharpen as each stroke becomes longer, deeper, and more forceful.

I cling to his powerful form, feeling the muscles of his back flex with each thrust of his hips into mine. His stav expands and he knots deep inside me, locking us together. A small pinch of pain turns quickly to bliss as his tip seals over my womb.

He stares down at me, his gaze fierce and possessive. "You are mine," he growls.

His words spark pleasure deep within as my body tightens around him. My head falls back and I cry out his name as my release roars through me.

He sinks his teeth deep into my neck as he claims me. Pain mixes with the ecstasy coursing through my veins.

The sting fades until I am only aware of the joining of our bodies. His stav begins to pulse in my core and he roars above me. "Mine!" Intense warmth erupts deep inside me, filling me with the delicious warmth of his seed.

He collapses on top of me, and I love the weight of his body over mine. He rolls us both onto our sides while he remains knotted inside me. He strokes my cheek and presses a series of tender kisses to my cheeks, nose, and brow before moving to my lips.

He rolls his hips against mine. "I want you again, my Lyana."

I seal my mouth over his, kissing him thoroughly. "I'm yours, my love."

EPILOGUE

CAELEN

When I awaken, Lyana is still asleep beside me. I curl my arm around her waist and pull her close as I gently nuzzle her hair. I splay my open palm over the slight swell of her abdomen and feel the life force of our child in her womb.

She turns in my arms to face me and presses a tender kiss to my lips.

"What shall we name her?" I ask.

She brushes the hair back from my face as she smiles. "You're so certain it's a girl?"

I nod. "Her life force is strong. She already reminds me of her mother."

"You will not be upset if we do not have a boy?"

"Never. Besides, this child is the first of many. We will have more than one son and daughter."

She laughs as I roll her beneath me, then arches a brow. "And just how many do you want, my love?"

I skim the tip of my nose alongside the bridge of hers

before capturing her mouth with my own. I pull back and kiss a trail across her jaw and down the elegant curve of her neck. She is more precious to me than anything, and I am addicted to touching her.

I lift my head and allow my gaze to travel over her lovely face. "As many as my beautiful wife will give me."

Her lips curve into a stunning smile. "I love you so much, my handsome High Elf husband."

I cup her cheek and stare deep into her luminous golden-brown eyes. "*Ashal'veh*, my lovely human wife."

ABOUT JESSICA GRAYSON

If you enjoyed this book, please leave a review on Amazon and/or Goodreads.

The next book in the series - ***Claimed By The Bear King: Bear Shifter Romance*** is available for preorder now.

Want more in this series ?

Fairy Tale Retellings (Once Upon a Fairy Tale Romance Series)

Taken by the Dragon: A Beauty and the Beast Retelling

Captivated by the Fae: A Cinderella Retelling

Rescued By The Merman: A Little Mermaid Retelling

Bound To The Elf Prince: A Snow White Retelling (This Book)

Claimed By The Bear King: Bear Shifter Romance

Protected By The Wolf Prince: A Red Riding Hood Retelling

Charmed by the Fox Prince: A Rapunzel Retelling

Oakvale Ever After series *is set in the same world as my Once Upon a Fairy Tale Romance series above.*

Kissing Potions and Elves

Enchanted Rings and Fae

Of Fate and Night Series

The Vampire's Bride

Of Fate and Kings Series

Bound to the Dark Elf King

Claimed by the Dragon King
Taken by the Fae King

Monster Brides Series
The Orc's Reluctant Bride

Do you like Dragon Shifters? Elves? Fae? Vampires?
Ice World Warrior Series
Claimed: Dragon Shifter Romance
Bound: Vampire Alien Romance
Rescued: Fae Alien Romance
Stolen: Werewolf Romance
Taken: Vampire Alien Romance
Fated: Dragon Shifter Romance
Protected: Dragon Shifter Romance

Want Dragon Shifters? You can dive into their world with this completed Duology.
Mosauran Series (Dragon Shifter Alien Romance)
The Edge of it All
Shape of the Wind

V'loryn Series (Vampire Alien Romance)
Lost in the Deep End
Beneath a Different Sky
Under a Silver Moon

V'loryn Holiday Series (A Marek and Elizabeth Holiday novella takes place prior to their bonding)
The Thing We Choose

V'loryn Fated Ones (Vampire Alien Romance)
Where the Light Begins (Vanek's Story)

For information about upcoming releases Like me on
  Facebook at Jessica Grayson
  http://facebook.com/JessicaGraysonBooks.

OR

sign up for upcoming release alerts at my website:
  Jessicagraysonauthor.com

ABOUT ARIA WINTER

Thank you so much for reading this. I hope you enjoyed this story. If you enjoy my writing, I also write under the pen name *Jessica Grayson*.

For information about upcoming releases Like me on Facebook (www.facebook.com/ariawinterauthor) or sign up for upcoming release alerts at my website:

Ariawinter.com

Want more Dragon Shifters? Check out my Beauty and the Beast Retelling below.

Once Upon A Fairy Tale Romance Series

Taken by the Dragon: A Beauty and the Beast Retelling
Captivated by the Fae: A Cinderella Retelling
Rescued By The Merman: A Little Mermaid Retelling
Bound to the Elf Prince: A Snow White Retelling (This Book)
Claimed By The Bear King: Bear Shifter Romance
Protected By The Wolf Prince: A Red Riding Hood Retelling
Charmed by the Fox Prince: A Rapunzel Retelling

Elemental Dragon Warriors Series

Claimed by the Fire Dragon Prince
Stolen by the Wind Dragon Prince
Rescued by the Water Dragon Prince
Healed by the Earth Dragon Prince
Chosen By The Fire Dragon Guard
Saved By The Wind Dragon Guard
Treasured By The Water Dragon Guard
Taken By The Earth Dragon Guard

Cosmic Guardian Series

Once Upon a Shifter Series

www.ingramcontent.com/pod-product-compliance
Lightning Source LLC
Chambersburg PA
CBHW020540020726
47494CB00006B/1846